SHERLOCK HOLMES
MYSTERY MAGAZINE

VOLUME 1, NUMBER 4   **WINTER 2010**

FEATURES

FICTION

CLASSIC REPRINT

POETRY

CARTOONS

"SOMEONE HAS KILLED THIS ANNOYING STREET MIME. IT COULD BE ANYONE IN LONDON."

Our cover this issue is by Chris Walker / www.eriboss.com

Publisher: John Betancourt
Editor: Marvin Kaye
Managing Editor: Karl Wurf

Sherlock Holmes Mystery Magazine **is published by Wildside Press, LLC. Single copies: $10.00 + postage. Subscriptions: $29.95 for the next 3 issues in the U.S.A., from:**
Wildside Press LLC, Subscription Dept.
9710 Traville Gateway Dr., #234; Rockville MD 20850

Ebook version available from Fictionwise.com & and other etailers.

FROM WATSON'S SCRAPBOOK

Welcome to the fourth issue of *Sherlock Holmes Mystery Magazine*. When this publication was initially planned, Wildside Press declared it would be carried on for four issues, after which it would be decided whether or not its reception by the reading public would merit it to be continued. I am happy to learn that a fifth number indeed will be produced, and am especially pleased to report that it will be an all-Holmes issue, a fact not without merit in terms of my friend Holmes's vanity.

Now Holmes and I have been deluged of late with a certain query, so before you ask, let me state that neither of us have seen, nor are likely to see, the new film starring that chap Downey as Holmes, and some bloke ostensibly portraying myself. It is Holmes's policy never to attend the theatre or the cinema if he is the principal subject of the plot. There was a time when he did, but it led to many occasions when he was expected to render an opinion of what he witnessed, and to do so objectively would be difficult, perhaps impossible, therefore he abstains.

I have no scruples in this regard. Successful films, books, plays, and of course this magazine, contribute healthily to my retirement income, inasmuch as they are all subject to royalties. (In this, I was quite delighted when copyright law was altered many years back to protect an author for life and many years after!) Another reason I try to stay current with the entertainment industry's ongoing fascination with matters Holmesian is that while my friend does not himself attend, he relies on me to report on what I've seen. (I suspect that when I render a positive opinion, he dons one of his disguises and goes incognito, but I cannot prove that.)

Over the years, my viewing experience has confirmed that I often come off better than Holmes does in the media, and a few examples immediately come to mind, though I think it impolitic to share them publicly. But in the case of the new film, I feel I owe an explanation for my decision not to watch it. Some months ago, I went to a theatre to see the latest Harry Potter installment. Before the feature began, there was the usual array of coming attractions (trailers I believe you Yanks call them) and one of them promoted the upcoming "Sherlockian" film.

Let me take a moment to state that Mr. Downey is an actor whose work I have always admired, and even in this instance I found him ever so likeable . . . but what in all good sense was the rest of that abominable nonsense about? I was frankly appalled both by the fragments of plot revealed in the trailer, and even more by the over-all tone of the proceedings. It was as incongruous to me as if I'd been invited to a Mozart concert and was subjected to Pink Floyd, instead.

I admit I may be unfair in what I feel here; films so often are better and quite different from the impressions conveyed by their coming attractions, but to quote that chap Han Solo, "I have a bad feeling about this." I leave it to our editor, Mr. Kaye, to weigh in on this issue.

—John H. Watson, M. D.

In deference to Dr. Watson's feelings about the new Robert Downey Jr. film, I decided not to take sides, but instead have asked one of our regular writers Bruce Kilstein to contribute a review of the new movie to *Sherlock Holmes # 4*.

This issue's nonfiction also includes a column by Lenny Picker and household hints from Holmes and Watson's erstwhile landlady, Mrs. (Martha) Hudson, plus an interview by Carole Buggé with Marina Stajic, chief toxicologist for the office of the New York Medical Examiner. Marina is an old friend of mine and Carole's; I first met Marina at The Wolfe Pack, the society devoted to

America's greatest (and largest) sleuth Nero Wolfe, though Marina considers herself more of a Holmesian aficionado.

Two Holmes stories are featured in this issue: Dr. Watson's own "Adventure of the Resident Patient" and "The Adventure of the Elusive Emeralds," a superb novella which Dr. W. generously enabled its author Carla Coupe to write from his original notes.

Literary associations infuse "Miss Podsnap's Pearls," a crime story by Roberta Rogow that involves one of the characters in the Charles Dickens novel, *Our Mutual Friend.*

"Another Night to Remember" and "The Man in the Overcoat" are more or less hard-boiled adventures. The first story, contributed by William E. Chambers, is reprinted from the 2004 Lawrence Block anthology, *Blood On Their Hands,* and the second is by Marc Bilgrey, *Sherlock Holmes Mystery Magazine's* regular cartoonist.

The issue is rounded out by Hal Charles's "Glass Eye," a new mini-mystery involving broadcast journalist and amateur detective Kelly Locke; a short-short by newcomer Melville S. Brown (thanks to Carole Buggé for recommending him to submit his story to *Sherlock Holmes Mystery Magazine*), and a rare foray into humorous fantasy by the late, lamented Jean Paiva.

Canonically yours,

Marvin Kaye

SHERLOCK ON SCREEN, AGAIN

by Bruce Kilstein

My recent trip to the theatre to see the new Sherlock Holmes movie confirmed why I like to read and write about Sherlock Holmes. I tried to attend the film with an open mind and cautioned myself not to let my personal, snobby, Conan Doyle-fundamentalist views of what Holmes "should be" get in the way of what may be a valid reinterpretation of the character and a potentially enjoyable entertainment experience. Reinterpretations of popular characters have been popping up in the movies lately, and some of them, like Batman and James Bond, seem to work well in their darker, introspective formats. The phenomenon of reinterpretation is by no means new to Sherlock Holmes, and, by some accounts, Holmes is the most reprised role in the history of film.

In 1903 American Mutoscope released "Sherlock Holmes Baffled," a 30-second film in which Holmes (played by an unknown actor) chases a ghost-like criminal with a bag of loot in someone's kitchen. It features trick photography and an exploding cigar. Later, we have Basil Rathbone and Nigel Bruce, who have become well-loved portrayers of Holmes and Watson in their films from the 1940's. While some of these films are based on Conan Doyle stories, others are contemporary interpretations set in World War II. One such example is "Sherlock Holmes and the Secret Weapon," wherein the brave duo must recover the stolen Tobel bomb sight, an invention, which, falling into Nazi hands could mean devastation for the good people of England. More on this in a moment.

Proper casting is critical to a film's success especially with a complex character like Sherlock Holmes. Correctly cast, Basil Rathbone *seems* like Sherlock Holmes to us, in part, because he meets our expectations portrayed in the original Sidney Paget drawings of Holmes in the *Strand Magazine*. Despite this, many odd casting decisions have been made in 200 or so Holmes films, for example, Peter Cushing and Christopher Lee, better suited for their classic portrayals of Dracula and Dr. Frankenstein in the Hammer films (of the two, Lee makes a better Holmes); or Roger Moore in "Sherlock Holmes in New York" with Patrick Macnee as Watson. Robert Duvall takes Watson to another level in "The Seven Percent Solution" (1976) and removes Watson from cartoonish sidekick to concerned friend and physician when he brings Holmes (played by the pasty Nicol Williamson) to see Sigmund Freud (Alan Arkin) for treatment for his cocaine addiction. In this film we are also introduced to Charles Gray playing Mycroft Holmes to such perfection that he is brought back to reprise the role 20 years later in the Granada TV series. Christopher Plummer and James Mason make an admirable attempt in 1979's "Murder by Decree."

In the above examples we see famous actors cast and miscast to play Holmes and Watson. Perhaps the best compliment for an actor is that we, the audience, get so absorbed in their portrayal of a character that we forget who the actor is. The flip side of this coin, the "worst compliment," is a situation in which we don't care who the actor is. Some of this, of course, has to do with the screenwriters. It is a struggle for a good actor to rise above a poorly plotted script dotted by vapid dialogue. It is an equal challenge for a great actor to blend his ego seamlessly into a well-drawn character. And so, we enjoy Basil Rathbone as Holmes even if he's in a heavy-handed war propaganda film, and we admire James Mason as Watson in a well-written mystery but can't seem to shake our image of him in "The Boys from Brazil" or "Heaven Can Wait." Rathbone *is* Holmes in a bad film, and Mason is … *Mason* in a good film.

Now, team up popular actors Robert Downey Jr. and Jude Law with action director Guy Ritchie ("Lock Stock and Two Smoking Barrels," Madonna's ex-husband), add 80 million dollars for special effects and computer-generated scenes and what do you get (besides three people who have all been arrested for assault)? An action/adventure film set in Edwardian London something like James Bond meets "National Treasure." The plot revolves around Holmes and Watson chasing after the snaggle-toothed Lord Blackwood (Mark Strong) as he uses black magic and secret rites in Harry Potter-style crypts to dominate a secret society, kind of like the Masons Gone Wild, in an attempt to use their power to take over Parliament and then … the world. As a sub-plot, not well-developed, Irene Adler (Rachel McAdams) returns from obscurity and, since she is the only woman Holmes has ever [allegedly! —*MK*] shown romantic interest in, is used as bait by Professor Moriarty (played by no one because he's always in the shadows) to manipulate Holmes and lead him to Blackwood's secret. Blackwood's secret is the employment of a good chemist and electrician to make magical effects and create a remote-controlled weapon that, if it falls into the wrong hands, could dominate the world (sounds awfully similar to the Tobel bomb sight from 1945, or any James Bond plot, for that matter). There is very little deduction and only a smattering of investigation on Holmes's part, but there is a whole lot of chasing and fighting; at least seven major fight scenes by my count. True, Holmes does have experience as a prize fighter ("Sign of Four") and as a practitioner of martial arts ('Baritsu' in "The Empty House"), but the current film imbues Holmes, Watson and Irene (!) all with super-human, ninja fighting powers. While the film was entertaining, I never felt like I was watching a Sherlock Holmes story.

There are nods to previous Holmes adventures, but these are frustrating. If you haven't read previous Holmes stories, you won't care about them; if you are a Holmes reader then you will be irked by their inaccuracy. For instance, Watson seems to limp around with the aide of a cane at times, referencing his wound in Afghanistan (see my story "Watson's Wound" in SHMM #3 for the "real" story) but the cane vanishes when Watson needs to leap about, fight villains and piggy-back Irene away from a potentially nasty encounter with a band-saw. Another oversight: Watson is engaged to Mary Morstan (Kelly Reilly) and Holmes makes an embarrassing scene at a restaurant when Watson finally gets his friend to meet his betrothed. The reader of Holmes knows that Watson met Mary when she was a client ("Sign of Four") and so had made Holmes's acquaintance when she met Watson. Further enraging the reader is Mary's comment to Holmes that she has read about the great detectives in the writings of Wilkie Collins and Poe, completely ignoring the fact that her fiancé has made Holmes famous by publishing the accounts of his cases.

Robert Downey Jr. cast as Holmes (we deduce something is afoot when we discover that his wife is one of the producers of the film) has the acting chops to explore the dark psychology of the detective, but his interpretation is more of Holmes as daredevil crazy person (more like his character Jim Barris in "A Scanner Darkly") rather than brilliant eccentric. Perhaps Downey is handcuffed by Michael Robert Johnson's script or Ritchie's vision for the film and simply has no leeway to interpret the role more intricately. Downey is also handcuffed to the bed by McAdams, who is cast as a young criminal of lower class than we would expect of Irene Adler, international seductress of royalty and Holmes.

This brings me back to why I and so many others like reading Sherlock Holmes. In the days before radio or TV or feature film, Conan Doyle invented a series of entertaining stories full of rich plotting and action, but most of all, he invented a character who could think. And while Sherlock Holmes can hold his own in fistfights, gun battles, dangerous animal attacks, poisonings and plunges over waterfalls, the action parts of the stories seem to be the framework, the bones that support the real meat of the drama: the process of deduction and investigation. We love being stunned by his minute powers of observation, which he reveals to an astonished Watson as "elementary." We enjoy his sarcasm when dealing with Lestrade, feel his pain at being a trapped intellect with little outlet for his talent, and are tormented when he plunges into the depths of drug addiction. We are cheered not because he catches the criminal but by his fierce loyalty to his friend. When Watson is shot in "The Three Garridebs," Holmes yells, "For God's sake, say you are not hurt!" Watson reflects that "it was worth many wounds to know the depth of loyalty and love which lay behind that cold mask."

Setting is important to any story and Conan Doyle froze a moment in history of late Victorian/Edwardian life that has disappeared. And so reading Sherlock Holmes is to step back into that time of wet cobbled streets, gas light, pipe smoke, hansom cabs and formal attire, and to explore the dark interiors from the drawing room to the slaughterhouse. I remember first reading the stories with a flashlight in the hall coat closet because it seemed like the proper, gloomy atmosphere (unless you have a study with a fireplace and a rainy afternoon handy). Perhaps this is why the Granada TV series with Jeremy Brett has become the iconic standard for screen versions of Sherlock Holmes where so many films have fallen short. In the television series, the viewer is rewarded by scenes that play out almost exactly as he/she has imagined them. One watches the episodes and says, "Yes, they got it right." The Guy Ritchie film does score points on the visuals, creating a very dark interpretation of 19th century London; you can almost smell the place oozing in creosote and feel the damp chill of the wind off the Thames. The score by Hans Zimmer is terrific as well, combining classical and English folk music for thrilling texture.

This is not to say that while we are comforted by Holmes fiction faithful to the Doyle Canon, we cannot be open-minded to exploration. I think that the TV series *House* is an example of using the characters of Holmes and Watson, re-imagined as Drs. House and Wilson, without trying to compete with Sherlock Holmes stories. The viewer gets mysteries to try to solve before the eccentric, brilliant, drug addicted (medical) detective can deduce the solutions, as well as the strong interplay between two friends. The setting works because we are not removing Holmes from his element, rather we are re-examining the two characters as archetypes. I think Doyle realized the depth that the exploration of friendship brought to the stories and he eventually killed off Mary Morstan so that Watson could move back in with Holmes. In *House*, Wilson's fiancée dies and we are glad to see Wilson and House sharing rooms again because we know how lonely each would be without the other.

It is interesting to note that where Hollywood has taken Sherlock Holmes in the direction of action hero and visual extravaganza, television writing has preserved the rich texture of the characters. I was pleased to learn that my nephew, Jackson, was Sherlock Holmes for Halloween this year (while it was the popular thing to be Spiderman, Batman, or one of the Incredibles) and has begun reading the Holmes stories. I won't tell him about reading in the hall closet; I'll leave it to him to discover his own dark places of investigation.

✗

A WOMAN OF HER TIME

by Carole Buggé

An Interview of New York City's Chief Toxicologist

"Conan Doyle? Oh, you mean Watson's literary agent?"

These words, from Marina Stajic, New York City's Director of Forensic Toxicology, greeted my question regarding the creator of the world's most famous consulting detective.

Marina Stajic is a self-described Sherlockian—but not just any Sherlockian. She is what the casual observer might define as "hard-core"—hence her response to my mention of Sir Arthur, delivered in the same dismissive tone of voice one might hear when uttering the phrase "theatrical agent."

Over mutton chops and ale at Keens Chophouse late one Wednesday night in February, I came to learn just how seriously Marina takes her devotion to the great detective. The night was cold, the fireplace at Keens was roaring, and the candlelight shone rosy on the fluted glassware of Marina's cosmopolitan. (I was drinking ale, but that struck me as much too mundane for her.)

Marina Stajic is an elegant woman of Yugoslavian/Jewish descent—although she is a longtime smoker, she looks much younger than her chronological age. Her voice is smoky, with throaty Eastern European vowels. Her impressive credentials as a scientist lend a kind of authority to her admittedly intense involvement with all things Sherlockian. As Marina herself puts it, "Never mind devout Catholics—Sherlockians are *serious*."

She is also a great storyteller.

Marina Stajic was born in Novi Sad, a town in Serbia on the Danube River, fifty miles north of Belgrade. It was part of the Austro-Hungarian Empire until the end of World War I, and she points out that there was a cultural difference between her hometown and the Turkish influence in Serbia proper. She liked chemistry as a child;

her first chemistry class was in the fifth grade in Yugoslavia. She still remembers thinking, "Chemistry will be really neat—physics will suck." Her interest was spurred on by wonderful chemistry teachers in grade school and high school, who influenced her to major in chemistry. (When pressed, she admits that her grandfather was a butcher in Yugoslavia, but insists that had little influence on her interest in forensics.) Her interest in crime, though, predated her interest in science. She liked crime fiction, and read translations in Yugoslavia.

Her first contact with Sherlock Holmes came in the summer of her thirteenth year. She was at a summer boarding school in Switzerland, and her best friend at school was from Afghanistan. Her friend's father was a military attaché in Moscow, and the two girls communicated in Russian, the only language they had in common.

One day, in a paddleboat on Lake Geneva, her friend told her the story of *The Hound of the Baskervilles*. She was captivated. As it happened, the movie version with Peter Cushing as Holmes and Christopher Lee as Henry Baskerville was playing at the time in the cinema, but the girls couldn't go because of the minimum age limit of seventeen! It's hard to imagine anyone censoring that, movies being what they are these days, but Marina had to wait until her seventeenth birthday to see the film.

However, that didn't stop her. She went home to Yugoslavia and went to the library and read every one of the Sherlock Holmes stories, starting with "The Hound of the Baskervilles," followed by "The Adventure of the Speckled Band." Her parents thought it was trash, and urged her to read *Heidi*, instead!

"You know, I feel there's actually a connection between Heidi and Holmes," she comments, leaning back in her chair as we order a second round of drinks. "They must have met in Switzerland around the time of the Reichenbach Falls adventure. They're about the same age." Not only that: Marina is convinced that they had an affair and that Heidi gave Holmes the idea of using the Baker Street Irregulars!

She also admires Agatha Christie, and points out that Christie's knowledge and use of poisons is better than Doyle's. "After all," Marina remarks, "she worked in the dispensary in World War I— all of her poison stories are very good."

Marina's first experience of the United States came at the age of fourteen, when she and her mother crossed the country by bus—99 days for $99 on Continental Trailways. They boarded the bus in New York City, and went nonstop straight to Phoenix, Arizona, and then onto Los Angeles. They returned the same way: it took them three days and nights going, and three days and three nights returning. They had breakfast at a diner, and were served the rest of their meals on the bus. It sounded grueling to me, but being from Yugoslavia, Marina says, the bus seemed to her like a luxurious way to travel—it actually had a toilet!

She eventually came to America for good, moving to Baltimore in 1972, where her brother was a Medical Examiner. Forensic toxicology was a developing field in those days, with very few women in it, and she immediately saw that it offered career possibilities. Other chemistry related fields were more saturated, so she settled on toxicology. She earned her PhD at the University of Maryland in Baltimore in forensic toxicology. In those days Baltimore was a rough town. "It became a better city after I left," she comments, "much as NYC became a better city after I moved here."

Her graduate school was close to "The Block" in downtown Baltimore known for all the strip joints—Belle Star even ran a place there. Edgar Allan Poe's grave was also only a couple of blocks away. Her school was in the downtown Baltimore campus of the University of Maryland, the main campus being in College Park, Md. The University of Maryland, she points out, has more campuses than any other university in the world.

After a stint working as a toxicologist in Virginia, in a suburb of Washington, D.C., she moved to New York City on April 1, 1986—"the year the Statue of Liberty was one hundred years old," she adds proudly. "In New York City I felt like I finally came home." She joined the Office of Chief Medical Examiner as Director of the Forensic Toxicology Laboratory, a position she still holds today.

When the subject of belief comes up, she shrugs. She's not an atheist or agnostic; she's a self-proclaimed "nothing." She simply isn't interested in the question. She claims to know what happens after you die, because it will be on Yogi Berra's tombstone: "It's over."

The closest thing she can think of to church is Yankee Stadium. "If I say I went to church, my friends say, 'Oh, yes, she went to the stadium.'" When the subject of Nero Wolfe comes up, she complains that the problem with Archie Goodwin is that he's not a Yankees fan. She points out that Conan Doyle actually went to a Yankees game against the Philly A's when he was in New York.

She smiles. "If there is a heaven I will be just one of the Yankee Stadium ghosts."

When asked about interesting cases in her past, she tells the story of the only truly Christie-like poisoning she worked on. It was in Virginia. She points out, murder by poison is not as common as it used to be ("because it's much easier to shoot someone.") Also, poisons are more controlled than they used to be.

It involved the death of an eighty-year-old man, who began feeling bad one day. He went to the hospital, where he subsequently died. The old gentleman was a widower and had been living with a woman who was thirty years his junior—in fact, he had children her age by his first wife. They lived on a farm outside of Washington, DC, and he had left the farm to her in his will.

His children by his first wife claimed it was murder, and that their 'stepmother' had killed him. Everyone doubted them, but they insisted, calling the pathologist who did the autopsy, claiming that their father was poisoned with rat poison. However, there was no indication of the presence of the usual suspects—anti-coagulants or cardiac glycosides—so poison had initially been ruled out. He didn't have bleeding, which would have been expected if anticoagulants were used and he had been in the hospital under observation for a whole week.

Finally, the pathologist agreed to further toxicology testing, "just to calm them down." He realized that the children were thinking of arsenic—which he considered highly unlikely—but he ordered the tests anyway. It turned out that the old gentleman was loaded with arsenic. The conclusion was that he had died from an overdose of rat poison. Fortunately, the police still had a garbage can with his vomit in it, as well as a bottle of Scotch from the house. They were both loaded with arsenic, an ingredient found only in older forms of rat poison.

When they confronted the "widow" with the toxicology results, she confessed at once. She admitted she didn't want to wait any longer to inherit the farm, and so had poisoned her common law husband. It seems that since it was an old farm, she had managed to get tins of old rat poison—hence the presence of arsenic. They got a conviction and she went to jail.

Marina also cited another interesting case in which a man poisoned his two year old child with benadryl. He claimed that the little girl got the drug from the medicine cabinet in the bathroom. He was careful enough to plant her footprint on the toilet seat underneath the medicine cabinet, but not smart enough to realize that she wasn't tall enough to reach it! As a result of his conviction on this case, an earlier case of a child he had suffocated was re-opened.

If these stories feel like they're right out of CSI or Forensic Files, it's no wonder. Marina and her colleagues actually do the things we watch the television scientists do: examine samples, run mass specs and high pressure liquid chromatographs. Perhaps it's not quite as glamorous as on television, but it's fascinating work nonetheless.

One can only imagine that Sherlock would be very impressed.

SCREEN OF THE CRIME

MAN OF THOUGHT, MAN OF ACTION, OR HOW <u>A STUDY IN TERROR</u> GOT THE BALANCE RIGHT (UNLIKE A CERTAIN OTHER FILM)

by Lenny Picker

A substantial portion of the by-no-means-universal adverse reaction to the 2009 movie *Sherlock Holmes*—both from Sherlockians as well as from lay viewers and reviewers—stems from its focus on portraying the detective as an action hero who in many respects resembles Batman, who also used his fists as well as his brain to combat crime. As an example, one of the opening scenes in the film, in which Robert Downey, Jr.'s Holmes analyzes the specific impact of his martial arts moves before immobilizing an opponent is, if not a conscious homage to, then a close parallel to a scene in a Frank Miller comic book, in which Gotham's protector does almost exactly the same thing. Even *The New York Times* editorial board, in opining on whether Holmes should be fully in the public domain, noted that "the master of the cerebral has been turned into an action hero" in the movie.

While I found the movie neither as bad nor as good as it could have been, I anticipate that fans of it who then turn to the Canon for more of the same will find Doyle's brilliant tales of scientific investigation disappointingly sedate. Despite thoughtful analyses by those such as Robert Davis ("Film Friday: Comparing Ritchie's *Sherlock Holmes* to Conan Doyle's Stories"), there's a difference between scattered references in the originals to Holmes mastering the Japanese art of baritsu, to his being a gifted amateur boxer, and to being a singlestick expert, and the long fight sequences in Guy Ritchie and Lionel Wigram's vision.

But as the Master himself quoted from Ecclesiastes, in *A Study in Scarlet*, "there is nothing new under the sun," (with the possible exception of a naked Holmes handcuffed to a bed by Irene Adler for no particularly good narrative reason). Almost half a century ago, another filmmaker sought to depict the sleuth as more of a man of action than had been the case in previous screen incarnations, and the publicity campaign for the movie even tried to appeal to the fans of the campy Adam West Batman TV series by using the slogan "Here comes the original caped crusader!" But in spite of the sensational and misleading tagline and a cheesy poster replete with sound effects rendered into words—"Biff!", "Crunch!", etc., straight from the television show, (presumably selected under the theory that salting the ads with "Observe", "Contemplate", and "Deduce" wouldn't pack the seats), the forces behind 1965's *A Study In Terror* convincingly integrated action and combat into a storyline true to the spirit of the detective Conan Doyle created, by making such scenes secondary to actual deduction. By doing so, they made one of the best-regarded, if least-known Holmes films of all time.

A Study In Terror broke ground on a number of fronts, most notably for pitting Holmes against Jack the Ripper on film for the very first time. While that concept may seem unremarkable today, given the 1979 movie *Murder By Decree*, and numerous pastiches (most significantly, Lyndsay Faye's 2009's standout *Dust and Shadow: An Account of the Ripper Killings* by Dr. John H. Watson), it was novel in 1965. And as Holmes was at the peak of his career during the 1888 Autumn of Terror during which the Whitechapel murderer operated, setting him on the serial killer's trail made perfect sense, as I argued in a 1981 article for the *Baker Street Miscellanea* ("A Few Words On Behalf of Jack the Ripper"). The panicked frenzy the Ripper created would not have allowed

Holmes to sit idly by, even if the savagery of the crimes differed from his usual case (a conclusion that rests on the good doctor's admitted exercise of discretion in determining which investigations conducted by his friend were fit for publication).

Its recent addition to Turner Classic Movies' roster (it debuted during the Christmas 2009 marathon) should give American audiences more opportunities to view it, despite its continued unavailability on DVD over here, notwithstanding reports that Sony was to release it in the fall of 2009. In my view, any serious admirer of the characters should seek it out, and Messrs. Ritchie and Wigram would be well-advised to widen their gaze to include it before beginning their already-green-lighted sequel that is expected to bring Professor Moriarty front and center, a storyline that cries out for a carefully-crafted battle of wits between intellectual equals, rather than focusing on fisticuffs. While *A Study In Terror* does have its flaws, they are relatively few, and more than outweighed by a stellar cast, superb pacing, and an intelligent script that seamlessly integrates quotes from the Canon, with clues as to the identity of the Ripper placed fairly before the viewer, while offering multiple suspects for consideration.

After three prostitutes are savagely slaughtered on the streets of Whitechapel, Holmes (John Neville) is sent an anonymous package addressed in "a female hand," containing a set of surgical instruments with the post-mortem knife removed, which nicely sets up the absence of something, rather than its presence, as a clue, in the spirit of the classic "the curious incident of the dog in the night-time," from "Silver Blaze." The case containing them provides a splendid opportunity for Holmes to demonstrate his deductive method. Holmes's careful examination of the object leads him to conclude that "[t]hese instruments belonged to a medical man who has descended to hard times," explaining to Watson (Donald Houston), portrayed here as a solid, dependable and intelligent companion, rather than Nigel Bruce's Boobus Britannicus, the logical basis behind his conclusion: that "the instruments of one's trade are always the last things to be pawned," and that the presence of a "fleck of white, silver polish," on one of the instruments shows that "they have been treated like common cutlery by someone concerned only with their appearance." The presence of a three-digit pawn ticket number in chalk on the outside of the case confirms his deduction.

Houston's Watson does not react with dumb-founded amazement; instead, he's comfortable challenging the conclusion, suggesting that the case could have been "stolen from a doctor and then pawned," a perfectly logical hypothesis that establishes from the outset that he will serve as an asset, rather than a liability to the inquiry to come.

Holmes responds by explaining why the doctor's theory is wrong. ("If the pawnbroker had thought they were stolen, he would never have displayed them in a window.")

But the hyper-intelligent Holmes is just getting started, astonishing Watson, and the viewer by declaring, with supreme self-confidence, "The shop faces south in a narrow street. And business is bad. I should also add that the pawnbroker is a foreigner."

When Watson starts to protest that he cannot see how Holmes reached these conclusions, Holmes impatiently cuts him off, "You see everything, but observe nothing," a combining of the lines from "A Scandal in Bohemia", "You see, but you do not observe," and, from "The Blue Carbuncle", "You can see everything. You fail, however, to reason from what you see." The master reasoner elucidates:

> Observe how the material has faded here. The sun has touched the inside of the case only when at its height, and able to shine over the roofs of the buildings opposite. Hence, the shop is in a narrow street, facing south. And business had to be bad for the case to remain undisturbed for so long.

He further points out that "the seven in the pledge number is crossed in the Continental manner," thus establishing that the pawnbroker was not British.

This initial depiction of Holmes is fully in the spirit of the Canon, echoing similar scenes of demonstrated brilliance in "The Blue Carbuncle," "The Norwood Builder," and *The Hound of the Baskervilles*. It portrays the character foremost as a man of intellect. In contrast, Downey's Holmes is first seen calculating the blows he will land on an adversary. Unfortunately, this sort of opening is a rarity. (The only parallel that springs immediately to mind from the big screen is Rathbone's Holmes accurately identifying personal details about Dr. Mortimer based on a study of the latter's forgotten walking-stick.) But perhaps this failing, is not, on reflection, surprising, given the thought needed to simulate the brilliant staccato deductions Doyle managed with apparent ease.

Holmes's further examination of the medical case finds that it bears the coat of arms of the Osbourne family, and the pair's visit to the family home yields the revelation that it had been given as a gift by Edward Osbourne, Lord Carfax to his older brother, Michael, who had been studying to become a doctor, over the objections of the Duke of Shires, his father, who considered the pursuit beneath the dignity of the family. The search for the missing eldest son and heir, and the connection between his property and the Whitechapel murders drives the rest of the plot, culminating in a taut and dramatic confrontation between detective and killer.

By seeking to attract the viewer to Holmes based on his amazing brain, rather than some other characteristic, the screenwriters, Donald and Derek Ford, ground the violence of their story firmly in tradition, insuring that it is not the tail wagging the hound. The movie's subject matter naturally lends itself to the inclusion of action scenes, but they are integral to the plot. After questioning a suspect, Holmes and Watson are set upon by thugs he dispatched out of a concern that they had learned too much about his illegal operations, a scene reminiscent of one in the Downey movie. As the death toll mounts, the pair take to the streets in an effort to find, as Holmes puts it, "the detail that matters," but are too late to prevent the murder of Mary Jane Kelly. But their proximity to the crime (in the movie's most serious departure from the historical record—the time between the murder and the Ripper's flight from Kelly's room is much too short to allow for the obscene surgery the killer conducted) allows Holmes to almost catch his man in a frantic and gripping sequence. There is also a fight sequence at the movie's end when he eventually traps his quarry.

Making a mystery more visually engaging on the screen by including such sequences is typical; for example, the Granada adaptation of "Charles Augustus Milverton," *The Master Blackmailer* expands on the Canon to include a fistfight between a disguised Holmes and his jealous rival. Rathbone's Holmes's first encounter with Moriarty in 1939's *The Adventures of Sherlock Holmes* ended in a wrestling match, obviously paralleling Doyle's own portrayal of their encounter at the Reichenbach Falls. And there's nothing inherently wrong with scenes of violent action—stories of armchair deduction such as "The Gloria Scott," or "The Veiled Lodger," are not the Canonical norm.

A Study In Terror also stands out with its superior ensemble cast, rivaled only by that of *Murder By Decree*, with whom it shares two members. Neville, best-known to modern audiences as The Well-Manicured Man of *The X-Files*, is one of my favorite Holmes—incisive, resourceful, and a sophisticated observer of human nature. His Holmes is capable of outrage and strong emotion, but he is more in control of himself than in Christopher Plummer's portrayal. He knows how to use his reputation to his benefit; his name alone is enough to intimidate witnesses. Unfortunately, he only played the part again as one of the successors to John Wood in the 1970s revival of the William Gillette play, and in an obscure CBC radio play, *The Incredible Murder of Cardinal Tosca*, whose script did not match his acting talent. We can only wonder what might have been had Neville not declined to succeed Douglas Wilmer in the 1960s BBC series that was eventually filmed with Peter Cushing in the part.

As noted, Houston continued in the footsteps of Andre Morrell as a serious Watson, foreshadowing similar approaches to the role by Robert Duvall, James Mason, David Burke and Edward Hardwicke. Inspector Lestrade, who in the Rathbone films managed the improbable feat of making Bruce's Watson look smart in comparison, finally got his due, thanks to Frank Finlay, who reprised the role in *Murder By Decree*. The movie also featured Dame Judi Dench in one of her first roles, as a young idealist running a mission in the East End, along with her uncle, portrayed by Anthony Quayle. And the movie's grimness, inherent in its subject-matter—the Ripper's gory assaults are not for the squeamish, even if the horrific mutilations are only alluded to—and its frank portrayal of mortuaries and the plight of the London underclass, is lightened intermittently by Robert Morley, whose delightful and charming portrayal of Mycroft Holmes was the first in an English-language talking picture.

My regard for the movie is not a blinkered one. The Ripper's reason for killing is not fully-developed. In contrast to *Murder By Decree*, Watson is, illogically, relegated to the sidelines for the unmasking of the killer, and the writers place Holmes in a deathtrap that they are not able to write their way out of. The soundtrack, perhaps the first ever released on record from a Holmes film, is uneven and sometimes jarring, and the real victims of the Ripper were not as healthy and well-nourished as portrayed in the movie, which does not concern itself overmuch with historical accuracy. But these are quibbles, at best. Neville and Houston deserved more outings in their roles, and forty-five years later, their performances, both individually and jointly, rank among the best in the history of Holmes on the screen. And the Fords and director Herman Cohen (also responsible for the giant gorilla movie, *Konga*) proved that an in-period Holmes movie not derived from the Canon could be done well.

By keeping Holmes the man of action in proper proportion to the thinker who could sit for hours, if not days, on end, developing and testing theories, Ritchie and Wigram could go a long way, in their next film, to allaying the qualms of many of their critics. *A Study In Terror* shows how to do just that.

A closing warning: *A Study In Terror* was subsequently novelized by Ellery Queen and Paul Fairman; its conceit was having Queen being sent Watson's manuscript and applying his own detecting gifts to ascertaining whether Holmes correctly identified the Ripper. The sections from Watson's journal have their moments, but I'd strongly recommend that the novel, which has been periodically reprinted in Ripper anthologies, be read only after seeing the movie.

✗

Lenny Picker, whose experience of things Sherlockian extends over four decades and three continents, stayed up until 4:00 a.m. while a teenager to catch *A Study In Terror* on *The Late Late Show*, in the days before VCRs and DVRs.

He can be reached at <chthompson@jtsa.edu>.

ASK MRS HUDSON
by (Mrs) Martha Hudson

Mrs Hudson,

The comings and going of our children at all hours, when they were in college, was exceedingly annoying. How do you deal with the peculiar, middle-of-the-night arrivals of desperate help-seekers wanting assistance from Mr Holmes? Are the renters of 221-A or 221-C upset? Do they protest? Or is that immaterial given the status of your most celebrated tenant?

John Jakes

Dear Mr Jakes,

First of all, thank you so much for your kind concern and realisation of my delicate and unusual position. A woman such as myself, raised in gentility and comfort, is not by nature accustomed to the odd array of rough trade, ragamuffins and ruffians who appear at our doorway all hours of the day and night.

In fact, I have lost a number of other tenants due to the professional activities of my most famous lodger. A certain Mrs Moynihan in 221-C was most disturbed by the series of random gunshots Mr Holmes was given to discharging whenever he felt like it. Dr Watson mentions this in his stories, but what he fails to mention is that the elderly widow living upstairs, already faint of heart and given to nervous palpitations, was driven to distraction by the unpredictable and unexpected blasts of gun powder from 221-B.

She complained to me, and Mr Holmes was persuaded to curtail his explosive enthusiasms. Dr Watson prescribed her valerian roots to help her sleep, but her nerves were quite frayed by that time, and she could not be persuaded that Mr Holmes had agreed to give up his odd habit. It seems the gunshots brought her unpleasant memories of her days in Ulster, also known as Northern Ireland, after the famine, during the "Troubles."

Dr Watson was kind enough to help her secure a very satisfactory set of rooms in Kensington, and Mr Holmes insisted on paying her first year's rent. So in the end, I felt she came away well enough, though I daresay she would have preferred not to move.

Then there was Mr Grieves in 221-A. He was a mild-mannered little man, a bookkeeper by trade, and kept very much to himself. He had a thin little mustache and kept a budgie in his bedroom in a gold cage, which he fed walnuts and raisin bread. He never said a word to me about Mr Holmes' odd parade of visitors until the day he ran into the baron in the hallway. It seems Mr Grieves didn't move out of the way fast enough, and the baron challenged him to a duel to satisfy his injured honour. He gave him a choice of pistols or rapiers, as I recall, and told Mr Grieves that his second would call on him at dawn the following Saturday.

Mr Grieves was gone by Thursday, and left no forwarding address. When the baron's second arrived on Saturday, he was surprised to be greeted by my newest tenant, a spinster schoolteacher from Tewkesbury. Needless to say, she did not accept his offer to defend Mr Grieves' honour—though I'm not convinced the second believed her assertion that she had never set eyes upon the unfortunate bookkeeper.

But even with all of this, I wouldn't trade my years with Mr Holmes and Dr Watson for anything. Dr Watson is the kindest and most considerate of men, and Mr Holmes, God bless him, has his ways of endearing himself to a woman such as myself. He can be brusque, of course, but when he takes the time to think about it, he is the most charming of men. And of course he is never late with his rent, pays in advance, and insists on giving me a "little extra" for groceries and the like from time to time.

I consider myself lucky to call both of these gentlemen not only my tenants, but—I flatter myself to think—also my friends.

Yrs Truly,
Mrs Hudson

*   *   *   *

Dear Mrs Hudson,

I am a landlady myself, and usually I have no trouble with my tenants. For the most part, they are a reliable and trustworthy lot, paying on time and doing their best not to damage my property.

However, about a year ago I had a dreadful woman—Kristin Halvorsen by name—who claimed to be an artist from Paris. She gave me a cheque which later bounced, and to top it off, she left the faucet on, creating a leak in the ceiling which I had to have repaired at my own expense. She left in the middle of the night, leaving me with an unpaid bill and an expensive ceiling repair.

Should I try to hunt her down or write her off as a bad experience? Any advice you have for me is much appreciated.

Sincerely,

Concerned in Cranleigh

Dear Concerned,

Write her off. If you believe in Fate, then this horrid woman will some day get what is coming to her. She may find herself confronted by a landlord someday who will recognize her for what she is, and, with any luck, end up in a gaol cell. It is my experience that people such as her trip up sooner or later.

Until then, don't waste any more time thinking about her. My dear sister used to say that everyone gets what they deserve in the end. I am not so confident in the divine justice of Providence, but I do believe in living for the joys in life. It is far too short to do otherwise.

Go out and buy yourself a new hat, some heavy cream, and make trifle tonight for pudding. It will make you happy, and your lodgers will love you for it. I have listed my own recipe for trifle at the end of this column.

Sincerely yours,

Mrs Hudson

*   *   *   *

Dear Mrs Hudson,

Ever since I was a child I have had a delicate constitution, and I am given to fainting spells, especially when attractive men are present. My sister claims I am pretending to faint, but I swear to you that is not the case.

It is very embarrassing—last week I fainted during Mrs Boyle's annual Christmas ball, and when I came to, I was in Mr Apthorp's arms. I was so mortified I pretended to swoon again, and begged to go home, just so I wouldn't have to face Mrs Apthorp on the dance floor. What can I do? I am already nineteen and my sister says I will never find a husband if I don't cure myself of this unwelcome affliction. I would be grateful for any advice you can give me.

Swooning in Swansea

Dear Swooning,

Loosen your corset two notches. And do not attend parties where there are handsome married men who are waiting to catch young girls who faint in front of them. Confine your swooning to places where only single young men are present, and you will find a husband within the year.

Yours,

Mrs Hudson

*   *   *   *

Dear Mrs Hudson,

I have a nervous stomach. I notice it is much worse when my husband is around, but since we're living in his mother's house, I don't imagine I'll be getting rid of the source of my stomach trouble anytime soon.

I would appreciate any advice you can give me.

Sincerely,

Bilious in Bathgate

Dear Bilious,

The most helpful advice I could give would be to replace either your husband or his mother, but since that is unlikely, here are the treatments for colic passed down to me from my Scottish grandmother:

In mild attacks, place hot cloths or a light mustard plaster upon the abdomen. Take a little Jamaica ginger in a tablespoonful of brandy or whisky, by the mouth. Chloroform may be administered, either by inhalation or twenty drops of it may be given in a little brandy. In most cases it will be desirable that the patient take some opium, not only to secure immediate relief from the spasm, but also to promote the evacuation of the bowels, which must happen before the patient will be entirely safe from a recurrence of the pain. Twenty drops of laudanum may be given, or if the patient be constantly vomiting, a teaspoonful of laudanum mixed with a little starch may be injected into the rectum. If the pain does not subside within an hour, this dose may be repeated.

A note about the opium: be very chary of this drug, as Dr Watson informs me that it is highly addictive in nature.

If there is no vomiting present, and the colic is the result of indigestion, an emetic should be administered in order to empty the stomach. The quickest, though not the most certain, way of securing vomiting, is to tickle the throat with the finger or with a feather; if this measure be not successful, half a tablespoonful of common salt or mustard may be dissolved in a glass of warm water and swallowed. This may be repeated in ten minutes if the vomiting be not induced within that time.

I hope you feel better soon.

Best wishes,

Mrs Hudson

* * * *

And now, readers, as promised, here is my recipe for Scotch eggs, a favourite of Dr Waton's, as well as my grandmother's recipe for trifle.

Mrs Hudson's Scotch Eggs

Ingredients:
6 hard-cooked eggs, well chilled
1 pound breakfast sausage
1/2 cup flour
2 eggs, beaten
3/4 cup fine bread crumbs
Vegetable oil for frying

Method:

Peel eggs and set aside. Divide sausage into 6 portions. Roll each egg in flour and with hands press a portion of the sausage around each egg.

Dip sausage-wrapped eggs into beaten eggs and roll in bread crumbs. Heat vegetable oil until just beginning to smoke.

Cook each egg in oil about 4-5 minutes or until sausage is cooked and browned. Drain on paper toweling. Serve warm. Serves six.

Grandmother McLaren's Trusty Trifle

Ingredients:

8 ounces fresh heavy cream, whipped
8 ounces container sour cream
1 (9 inch) angel food cake or sponge cake or lady fingers
1 cup vanilla pudding, homemade from fresh egg yolks
8 ounces sweet cherries, peeled and sliced
1 pint fresh strawberries, sliced
3 bananas, peeled and sliced
10 ounces crushed pineapple, drained
1 sprig fresh mint
4 ounces rum

Method:

In a medium bowl, fold sour cream and pudding into the whipped cream.

Cut the cake into thirds, horizontally.

Line a large trifle or other glass serving bowl with cherries and strawberry slices. Place one layer of cake or lady fingers in bottom of bowl, top with 1/3 of bananas and pineapple, and 1/3 of whipped topping mixture. Repeat layering until all ingredients are used.

Make fan garnishes of whole strawberries by slicing from just below the stem. Garnish assembled trifle with fanned strawberries, and a sprig of mint. Refrigerate until serving. Drizzle with rum just before serving.

✗

THE BITTER HALF

by Stan Trybulski

I

Mike Shanahan's predilection for publicity was a legend in the law enforcement business. He wore it with undisguised pride, as if it were a cluster of battle ribbons instead of just a fat collection of news articles hung on the walls of his office, only waiting for the next visitor to goggle over. During his twenty-three years with the New York City Police Department he had never been shy about promoting his collars, so that when he was selected to become the new Special Commissioner for Investigations of the New York City Board of Education, he carried a vast network of personal press contacts with him.

Now, ensconced in a large corner office on the twenty-second floor of a downtown office building, Shanahan could take breaks from the tedious rigors of his position by gazing out of his large windows at Manhattan and the City—his City.

A receptionist with close-cropped blonde hair that allowed her to display a pair of diamond-studs in her ear lobes was well-protected by a thick layer of architectural safety glass. She looked up from her computer and buzzed me in as soon as I stepped out of the elevator. I was expected, so it seemed. She offered me a seat on one of the plush leather chairs in the outer office and remarking on the August heat, asked if I would like some water. I told her no and she picked up the phone on her desk and spoke softly into it. Then she turned her attention back to the computer screen in front of her and began playing with the electronic mouse. I looked down at the plush beige carpeting and listened to the quiet hum of the central air conditioning. Having my fill of the carpet, I looked out past the architectural safety glass at the elevator foyer with its rich, mahogany stained paneling and recessed soft lighting. Then I listened some more to the hum of the air conditioning. After a while, I looked at the wall behind the receptionist. There was a large color photograph of Shanahan and the mayor, smiling and shaking hands. I guessed he wanted visitors to know right off the bat where he stood—and they stood. I am power.

I was back staring at the beige carpet and thinking about that and wondering why he had asked me to come down to his office and meet with him when a door in the mahogany-paneled wall popped open and a heavyset man with a shaved head glanced at me.

"Doherty?"

I nodded my head.

"Let's go, the Commissioner's waiting."

The blonde receptionist looked up at me and smiled.

I followed the husky man down a long hallway, carpeted in the same plush beige as the reception area. At the end was another open area with a large desk and a young black woman with designer glasses and a blue silk pants suit sitting behind it.

"Is he on the phone?" the husky man asked her.

The young woman glanced down at the phone bank on her desk and shook her head.

Motioning for me to follow, the husky man opened the door and went in.

The office was large, long would be a better word, with a huge mahogany desk with a leather bordered ink blotter, phone bank, a copy of the *Wall Street Journal* and a thin manila folder on it. There were no ink stains on the blotter and the *Journal* appeared to be well-thumbed. There was a pair of leather captain's chairs in front of the desk and a huge executive chair behind it. The walls were paneled in a rich walnut and a mahogany credenza lined one wall and a long burgundy Chesterfield sofa was backed up against another. Ready, in case Shanahan needed to think.

Shaded light from a large smoked-glass picture window filtered across the room, only broken by the elongated shadow of Shanahan who was looking out over the skyline at the City. His city. On the East River, I could see the Brooklyn Bridge and beyond that span, the Manhattan Bridge. His bridges.

"Doherty is here, Commissioner," the husky man said, and left, closing the door behind him.

Shanahan didn't move, kept looking out the window at the view. The sun was high and the summer air surprisingly sharp and clear. He was making the most of the moment. I took a seat in one of the captain's chairs and waited.

"You wanted to see me?" I said after a long moment.

Finally, he turned and looked at me as if he was realizing for the first time that I was sitting there.

I glanced at my watch.

Shanahan ignored my gesture. "It's a magnificent view, don't you think?"

"Magnificent," I said. "Is that why you asked me to come down here, to enjoy the view with you?"

He laughed. It was hearty laugh, an infectious, I'm on your side, boys, laugh.

I didn't laugh with him. I knew bosses like Shanahan were never on my side.

He walked over to me, a big smile still on his face, and extended his hand. I stood politely and shook it. His grip was warm, political, just like his laugh.

"Good to see you again, Doherty. I don't think we've ever had the pleasure of really conversing together."

"Well, this is the first time I've ever been down here on unofficial business. Usually, I'm trying a case with your investigators."

"Ah, the daily grind," he said, pushing out a soft chuckle, waving his hand for me to sit back down. He went around to his side of the banquet table he called his desk and eased his six-two frame into the executive chair. His face was well-tanned and unlined, making him look twenty years younger than the just over fifty I knew him to be. His hair was exquisitely barbered with a part on the left side and he was wearing a lightweight three piece dark wool suit. I knew that even in this summer heat, he'd be cool. Guys like Shanahan always are. His shirt was white and unwrinkled and framed by a blue silk tie with a pattern of silver sailboats. Like his bridge and his city, I just knew the Atlantic was his ocean.

He gestured over at the credenza where there was a small pile of trial folders. "I spent the morning reading through the files of the cases that you've tried for us," he said. "You know, Doherty, despite the fact that you were never with the Manhattan D.A.'s office, you do good trial work. You're tenacious … and quick on your feet. I like that. And you spend a lot of time preparing your cases for trial."

"You can do that when you don't have anything else on your desk."

"Such is the life of an attorney in private practice." He shook his head slowly. "Well, maybe ..." he let the words drift slowly across the desk, then continued easily. "Perhaps, we can help you with that. The reason I asked you to meet with me, we have a case that might best be suited to an attorney with your strengths."

"Which would be?"

Shanahan rubbed his chin. "To be blunt, you no longer work for the City. You're an outsider. And that's a good thing. This case is a highly sensitive matter, otherwise I would have just referred it along the usual channels. The parent involved, however, is very high profile and very powerful and he's a valued friend of the mayor."

"He?"

"I'm going to introduce you to him in a few minutes. This is a missing witness case, the kind you've had some familiarity with, I believe. His daughter's been abducted."

Outside, the view was truly magnificent, Shanahan had been right about that; the sky was eggshell blue and the sunlight gleamed off the stainless steel frames surrounding the smoky glass of the skyscrapers, and all the cars on the Brooklyn Bridge looked like ants scurrying to and fro. The day was just too nice for me to sit here and let Shanahan shovel me a bucket of bull.

So I said, "I thought you said this was a missing witness case? If the girl's been abducted, why hasn't her father reported it to the police or the FBI?"

"Well ... it's not exactly an abduction." Shanahan leaned back in his executive chair. "It's not a kidnapping, maybe not even a crime; as a matter of fact, the mother may have taken the little girl. The parents have separated and are going through a nasty divorce and custody is an issue. I'm sure you've read about it."

"Not unless the story is sandwiched in between the race results at Saratoga."

Shanahan ignored my remark and continued. "So Mr. Stevens really doesn't want the authorities involved. He is desperate to avoid any more adverse publicity."

"Stevens?"

Shanahan sat up and lightly brushed the side of his head. "Oh, I didn't tell you his name, did I? It's Armstrong Stevens ... the Third. I'm sure you've heard of the financial firm of Morton Stevens."

I had. Who hadn't? One of the largest investment banking firms in the world. They had their fingers in every financial pie, whether half-baked or fully-cooked. But while I was impressed, I wasn't convinced.

"So why doesn't Stevens hire a professional security firm to retrieve his daughter?"

"The better the firm, the more resources. The more resources, the more personnel. The more personnel, the greater the chance that the news will leak out. It's as simple as that."

"As simple as that."

Shanahan nodded. "And Stevens is a very close friend of the Mayor, and his wife is a trustee of the Metropolitan Museum of Art. She's also an expert in Korean art. Very high profile people."

My turn to nod. "Therefore, the Mayor has come to you?"

He laughed slightly. "It seems that for all their wealth and connections, the Stevenses believe in public education. No Philips Exeter or Choate Rosemary Hall or Miss Porter's for their darling little princess. No, PS 41 in Greenwich Village is good enough." He shook his head and laughed again.

"So where does the missing witness angle come in?" I was curious now.

"Apparently the little girl—Suzie—Suzie Stevens was walking down the corridor when she saw a hypodermic needle fall out of a teacher's handbag. And she mentioned it to another girl who told her mother. And the mother called the principal . . ."

"And the principal called you." I cut him off. "How old is the girl?"

"Seven."

"So it's her word against the teacher's? Tough case to bring charges that will stick. They'll say she's making it up."

"Except that she's a Stevens. Hard put to show a reason for her to lie." He leaned forward and flipped open the thin manila folder. "Here's her description. Light brown hair with hazel eyes, just under four feet, thin but not skinny, last in school on May twenty-third, wearing tan slacks, a red blouse and red and blue swoops, not the fancy kind. Seems she was waiting at the entrance for the chauffeur to pick her up when Mrs. Stevens arrived in a silver Lexus. The girl ran toward the open door and got in. Hasn't been seen since."

"That's almost two months ago," I said. "Why the delay in looking for her?"

"Stevens figured as long as she's with her mother, she would be safe. But he hasn't heard from his wife all this time and now he's very worried. So worried he went to the Mayor for help."

"And billionaire to billionaire, the Mayor couldn't refuse, of course."

"Something like that, I suppose." He slid the manila folder over to my side of the desk.

I let it lie there. "So why me?"

He rubbed his chin. "As I said, you've done good work for us in the past ..."

"And you don't want your staff involved."

"The Mayor thinks it would be better that way." He took a deep breath. "This case could do a lot for you, Doherty. What do you clear now, handling misdemeanor cases, maybe three or four felony trials a year? Five, six thousand a month? We could triple that if this works out."

"What? Come to work for SCI?"

"No, but the Department of Education has a large legal staff. Think of that. Better money, a health plan, nothing too taxing, lots of time off, and a hefty pension at the end. You know you're not getting any younger."

"You make it sound like heaven." He was giving me the soft sell, sweet and slow. I wondered how he'd sound if I said I wasn't interested. But I knew I'd never find out. I had two mortgages to pay—one for the apartment in Brooklyn Heights, one for the country house; a car note on the Porsche I never should have bought, two cats to feed and rent on my office space downtown. I was doing better than Shanahan supposed, but not that much better that I could afford to turn him down.

"Let's back up a little ways," I said. "You mentioned a divorce action. Won't Mrs. Stevens eventually have to show up in court? Stevens could make a big stink with the judge."

"Eventually. That's the key word, Doherty. No one has seen hide or hair of her or the little girl except ..." He tapped the manila folder and arched his eyebrows.

I picked the folder up. Inside were three typewritten pages, single-spaced on plain paper with no letterhead. I glanced at them quickly. There was the description of little Suzie that Shanahan had just read to me as well as the details of her supposed abduction, including a synopsis of an interview with the teacher who witnessed the girl getting into her mother's Lexus along with a complete description of the car and its license plate number.

A brief discussion of Armstrong Stevens III followed. While his grandfather had been a founder of Morton Stevens and Armstrong had inherited a sizable chunk of the corporation's stock, he was not involved in the firm's business. Instead, he ran a private commodity investment fund, speculating in gold, oil and just about every raw material it was possible to wring a quick buck out of. He had offices in New York, Hong Kong and Bermuda and the report listed the addresses and phone numbers for all of them. I folded the sheets of paper up and put them in my jacket pocket and slid the folder back across the desk.

"Can I speak to Stevens?"

"He's here now, waiting in the conference room."

I followed Shanahan through a side door and into a long room with a large table and a dozen comfy leather chairs. The room was also richly paneled in dark wood and lush drapes covered a bank of windows, giving everything the air of hush-hush secrecy. He walked over to the chair at the end of the table and said, "Mr. Stevens, this is Doherty, the attorney I told you about."

The man seated on the end chair looked up at me, his well-tanned face lined with worry. His hair was close-cropped, graying at the temples and he sported a salt and pepper mustache, clipped to a military trim. His jaw was prominent, almost commanding and his lips were set with a firmness that undoubtedly devolved from his blue blood. Stevens was dressed for the summer weather in a striped seersucker suit and white shoes. Even though it was against the law in New York City to smoke in public buildings, there was a lit Churchill resting in an ashtray next to him.

Stevens picked up the cigar and puffed on it. When he exhaled, tiny wisps of smoke circled and climbed in tribute toward the ceiling air-conditioning.

"My little Suzie will be eight in a few weeks," Armstrong Stevens III said to no one in particular, looking at the cigar in his hand. "I don't want to miss her birthday."

His speech had that amorphous Continental tone that the East Coast Brahmins sometimes would pick up through cultural osmosis, usually leaving the cultural part behind. I sat down next to him and pushed the ashtray to the other side of the table.

"I'll leave you both to talk," Shanahan said as he opened the door to his office. I watched him step inside and close the door without a sound.

"I want to know more about your wife," I told Stevens.

He took another puff on the Churchill and set it back down in the ashtray, exhaled slowly and gazed at me with ice blue eyes, as if he was seeing me for the first time. "Do you want names? I could call her plenty, half of them would be true, half of them false. The problem, Mr. Doherty, is that I wouldn't know which are which. The closest I could come to an accurate description would be to say that she's my bitter half. Before Suzie disappeared, I was sure our attorneys would work out everything with the best interest of the child in mind. But I guess that's out now, with Andorra having run off with her."

"What have your attorneys said?"

He glanced at the manila folder in my hand. "I told them what I knew and they made some brief, very discreet inquiries. You have the report in your hand."

I opened the folder and looked at the top page of the report. "It's not on any law firm letterhead," I said.

"As I said, my attorneys are very discreet. They adopted the position that if I didn't want to take up the matter in court or hire an investigative agency, there was little else they could do."

"Do you think your wife has left New York? This could be an interstate matter; the FBI might take it over."

Stevens picked up the cigar and puffed again. "Mr. Doherty, if I had wanted the FBI involved, I could just pick up the phone and call Washington."

I nodded. I knew that when he said Washington, he meant the White House. And Stevens knew that I knew it.

"Could this be about money? Is your wife trying to hold you up?"

Stevens laughed. "Andorra was a Winstead before she married me. Does that mean anything to you?"

I shook my head. "Should it?"

He laughed again, a bitter tinge to the sound this time. "Her ancestors didn't just come over on the Mayflower, they owned it; her blood is bluer than blue with a dozen generations of amassed New England mercantile wealth to keep it pumping. She's as well-off as I am. No, it's not about the money, it's about power, control. As I said, she's my bitter half."

"Was the marriage always like this?"

Stevens set the cigar back down on the ashtray and fell silent. After a while, he said, "No. Funny thing, in the beginning, it was love, real love. But somehow we grew apart, I was spending more time on business and Andorra had the museum and her art connoisseurship. She's an expert in ancient Korean art, did you know that?"

He said that last bit with obvious pride in his voice and I wondered where the love had gone. And when.

"Do you think she might have taken Suzie to Korea?"

Shock registered on Steven's face, as if the idea was brand new to him. "Gosh, Mr. Doherty, I hope not. The teacher who saw them leave said Andorra had recently talked about spending several weeks up in Newport, at her family's summer cottage. She inherited the place when her mother died."

I opened up the folder and glanced at the second page of the report. The teacher, a Ms. Padavan, stated that she had overheard Andorra Stevens talk about Newport and sailing.

"How would this Ms. Padavan overhear your wife's conversations?"

Stevens blinked. "Oh, she was also tutoring Suzie in French; they were specializing in nineteenth-century poetry. She was often at our Park Avenue place."

"You mean you and your wife still live together, even though you're going through a divorce?"

"It's not as strange as it sounds, Mr. Doherty. The Park Avenue apartment is a duplex with fourteen rooms. I also spend a significant amount of time in my Hong Kong and Bermuda offices, and when I'm in New York, I stick to my floor and Andorra stays on hers."

"And little Suzie?"

"She has the run of the house, of course."

I looked at the report again. "It says here that Ms. Padavan thought she saw your wife on the Upper East Side recently."

Stevens puffed his cigar. "Thought she saw Andorra's Lexus to be more exact, and a woman driver who looked somewhat like my wife."

"So New York City would be a good place to start?"

"You tell me, you're the professional."

I didn't want to argue the point with him, I needed the dough and I didn't want to talk myself out of a lucrative case. Turning to the end of the report, I fixed my eyes on an eight-by-ten color glossy of a young brunette whom I took to be little Suzie. She was standing at the wheel of a handsome sailing yacht, her father holding her up while she steered. She was dressed in a blue blouse and white shorts and a navy sailing cap. I slid the photo over to Stevens.

He smiled as he looked at it. "I took this last winter at our cottage on Anguilla. She looks the same now, maybe a tad taller."

I took the photo back. "I'll need the name of your law firm; I'll have to speak to them."

"Pushkin and Salz. They're matrimonial attorneys. I've already alerted Tony Pushkin that you'll be by to see him."

"You're pretty sure of yourself, aren't you?"

"In my line of work I have to be."

"Is there a number I can reach you directly if I have to?"

Stevens took out a gold plated pen from his inside left breast pocket and jotted down a number on the back of the manila folder. "Only call if it's really necessary, I'm a very busy man."

"Only if it's necessary," I repeated.

Shanahan was looking out the window when I went back to his office.

"Still magnificent?" I said.

He turned to me. "So Doherty, will you help Mr. Stevens?"

"And you and the Mayor. Yeah, but we're talking trial rates. Fifteen-hundred a day and I want some upfront money for expenses."

"You understand that there can be no paperwork, no usual retainer agreement."

"I trust you."

"A matter of professional courtesy, then?"

"No, this is too big for you to try and screw me. But I want the upfront money now."

Shanahan went to his credenza and opened a door to reveal a small safe. Twisting the dial, he popped it open and brought a thick brown envelope over to his desk. He took out a stack of hundred dollar bills and spread out five evenly on the blotter, as if he was a casino blackjack dealer paying off a winning gambler. He didn't know how close to the truth that was.

"Five hundred. That should last you a couple of days."

I scooped up the bills and stuffed them in my trousers pocket. "Do you want a receipt?"

He shook his head. "Like I said, nothing on paper."

Pushkin & Salz had their offices on the eighth floor of an old building near Hanover Square. I walked down there from Shanahan's digs and was sweating heavily by the time a red-headed receptionist in black toreador pants, black silk blouse and stiletto shoes escorted me into Tony Pushkin's office. Pushkin was a pudgy middle-aged man with a sharply receding hairline above a florid, lined, overworked face. There was a tuna salad plate and an unopened bottle of seltzer on his desk. He was dressed in a tan linen suit and white shirt, but with no tie, he wasn't greeting a client.

"Doherty," he groused as he extended his hand. The grip was limpid, disinterested.

After we were seated, he continued. "Mr. Stevens has asked us to extend every courtesy to you."

"And his wish is your command."

"Something like that." He gestured at the manila folder I was still holding in my hand. "You have our report, I don't know what else I can tell you."

The air conditioner hummed. I said, "What about his firm's finances, business dealings? Anything that might concern Mrs. Stevens?"

Pushkin smiled wanly. "I'm afraid those affairs are handled by another law firm. We're strictly matrimonial. And what we don't know can't hurt our client."

The air conditioning was humming louder. "Or your firm," I said.

"You catch on quickly, Doherty. Ever thought about doing divorce work?"

"I'd rather drink rat poison."

Pushkin laughed. "It's not everybody's cup of tea, that's for sure." He stabbed at a piece of tuna with his fork and popped it into his mouth, chewed and swallowed.

"Yeah, it takes a special kind of lawyer," I said.

"That it does," he said, spearing some more of the fish. "Dealing with cheating spouses, kids in therapy, hidden assets, he said-she said. Every day of the week."

"It's a tough life."

Pushkin looked at me for a moment, trying to figure out if I was being sarcastic, then ate another forkful of tuna.

"Was Mrs. Stevens cheating on her husband?"

"Not that we know of," he said.

"What about him?"

Pushkin unscrewed the bottle top and drank some of the seltzer, and then wagged his finger at me. "That's a no-no. Attorney-client privilege. But I'll say this, he's married to his job."

"What about the little girl?"

"Sweetest kid you'd ever want to meet. Loves both her parents, though I don't know why."

This wasn't getting me anywhere so I changed tack and asked about the schoolteacher Padavan. He told me one of his young associates, Conrad Rivers, had interviewed her. He buzzed the receptionist out front. "Ms. Palmeri, tell Conrad to come to my office right away."

While we waited for Conrad, Pushkin attacked his salad, finishing off the slices of hard-boiled eggs, then the rest of the tuna and the tomato. He left the lettuce untouched.

The door opened and a tall, gawky kid walked in. He was wearing a blue button-down shirt and tie. The shirt had large circles of sweat stains under the armpits and the kid smelled with the perspiration of fear.

"You wanted to see me, Mr. Pushkin?"

"Conrad, this is Mr. Doherty. He's working for Mr. Stevens. Tell him what you know about the schoolteacher, Padavan."

"Not much to tell," the kid said.

"Probably not, but I want to hear it, anyway."

"I spent an hour with her at her place. Lives in a brownstone on West Eighty-Fourth Street. Said she witnessed the abduction, got the make, model and license plate. Said she saw Mrs. Stevens, or rather thought she saw Mrs. Stevens uptown a couple of weeks ago, driving away from an art gallery. Said she recognized the car, had seen it lots of times. All of this is in the report."

I stared at the kid. "No, it's not."

"Whaddya mean it's not?" Pushkin's question was a low growl.

I handed him the folder. "There's nothing in this about an art gallery, or that Padavan had seen the car previously on numerous occasions, so she'd be sure to recognize it."

Pushkin opened the folder and read the contents. Then he slowly closed the folder and set in on his desk. He threw Conrad a look that caused the kid's face to become ashen and the sweat stains on his shirt to widen.

"Jeez, Mr. Pushkin, I didn't think every detail was important."

"That's why I'm here," I told him. "Anything else that you left out of the report?"

Conrad rubbed his eyes and thought real hard. "No, that's it."

"Did you go to the art gallery and speak to someone?"

The kid turned even paler and shook his head.

I took the photo of Suzie Stevens out of the folder and asked Conrad to run off a stack of fifty copies. I sat there, trying not to be disgusted.

"He's my sister's kid. Just out of law school. What can you do? I can't send him into court, he'd stink the place up, so I figured he could handle a simple interview."

I looked at him.

He wiped his mouth with a paper napkin. "No harm done, right?"

"No harm done."

"You don't have to tell Mr. Stevens, do you?"

"Nah. Now tell me about Stevens cheating on his wife."

2

My usual table by the front window at McSorley's was vacant, a reserved sign sitting on its scarred wooden top. I sat down and signaled to Richie the waiter to bring two light ales and my laptop computer, which I kept stored behind the bar. I needed to think and ale was the best lubricant to keep the wheels turning. Outside, the sun was beating down on the pavement and shirtless hardhats were busy tearing down a building across the street. Soon, another structure, a modern monstrosity with million-dollar condos, would be born. When Richie brought me the holy waters and my laptop, I asked him to also bring me a cheddar cheese plate and handed him one of the c-notes Shanahan had given me.

"What'd you do, hit a long shot?"

"No, but thanks for the idea."

After Richie went off to serve some other tables, I logged onto the computer and went to the *Daily Racing Form* website. Scrolling down the listings for today's races at 'Toga, I stopped at the tenth race. It was an optional claimer on the inner turf with superfecta betting and Jean-Luc Samyn was riding a longshot called Patria o Muerte. Samyn on the green was the saying. So I wrote down six combo bets keyed around Jean-Luc's horse. There was a payphone next to the table, but I went outside and used my cell phone to call my regular bookie, Sonny HaHa in Queens.

When I returned, my plate of cheese and onions, a package of saltines and my change was waiting. Minnie and Stinky, the two gargantuan house cats that actually ran the establishment, were prowling back and forth along the sawdust covered floor.

I ate some of the cheese, slipping a slice to the cats, and drank my ale. Finishing, I signaled to Richie for more ale. He brought two frothy mugs and cleared away the table. The felines, realizing that my largesse was spent, trotted off after him. Alone again, I decided to Google all the sailing clubs in the metropolitan area. I came up with a list of forty-seven, including Long Island and New

Jersey. Between sips of ale, I went outside and called the telephone numbers on the list, asking for a Mrs. Stevens, insisting she must be there and describing her and little Suzie.

Two hours and eight ales later, all I had to show for my effort was a swollen bladder.

After a trip to the men's room, I came back to the table and decided to work a new angle. But first I had to think of one. Two ales later I tried the number listed in the report as belonging to Janet Padavan. A sugary female voice answered.

"Janet Padavan?"

"Yes. Who's calling?"

"My name is Doherty and I'm working for Mr. Stevens. Mr. Pushkin's associate, Conrad Rivers, said he has spoken with you about the abduction."

"Abduction? Oh my gosh, is that what it is?"

"It could very well be. I'd like to talk to you about the woman who looked like Andorra Stevens, the woman you say came out of the art gallery on the Upper East Side."

"She didn't look like Andorra Stevens. It was Andorra Stevens. I've been in their home at least a dozen times and I've also met and talked with her at school functions."

"You saw her come out of the gallery?"

"Well, not exactly. Her Lexus was parked right outside and I saw her pulling away from the curb."

"So what makes you think she was in the art gallery?"

"I was on foot and I couldn't follow her to be sure it was her so I went into the gallery and said I was there to meet Mrs. Stevens. The sales assistant said she had just left. I asked for her address but all they had was the apartment on Park Avenue."

"Did she purchase anything?"

"No. Funny thing, the manager said she was considering selling a few of the minor pieces in her collection."

"Collection?"

"Oh, didn't you know? Mrs. Stevens has one of the largest private collections of Korean art in the world. Much of it is on loan to museums but I've seen beautiful objects in her home. Really beautiful."

"No, I didn't know."

"Maybe, I've been of some help then."

"Yes, you have," I replied. "Thank you, Ms. Padavan."

"Call me Janet, I'm a friendly sort of person."

"Okay, Janet. I'm also a friendly sort person. You can call me Doherty."

The sun had moved to the west, creating a reddish hazy sky. The air was heavy and I was sweating bullets. Back inside McSorley's, two more ales cooled me off. I couldn't think of anything further to do on the case so I went back to my apartment, stopping at the Chinese restaurant around the corner. While they cooked some shrimp in chili sauce to go, I called my service to see if the courts had any assignments for me. Nada. Upstairs, I ate and watched the news, hand feeding slices of shrimp to Momma Sweet and Diva, my number one and two cats.

I was about to turn in when an idea hit me. I picked up my phone and punched in the numbers for the Stevens' home.

A young female voice answered.

"Good evening," I said. "This is the McSorley's Gallery. We're trying to reach Mrs. Stevens about some objects she may wish to sell. Is she available?"

"I'm sorry. Mrs. Stevens is out of town."

"Is there any way she can be reached?"

"No. I'm sorry."

I thanked her and hung up. Then I punched in the numbers for the Winstead cottage in Newport. This time a man answered and I ran down the McSorley's gallery spiel I had come up with a few minutes ago.

The voice told me in a clipped English accent that Mrs. Stevens was not occupying the premises at the moment and that he had no way of getting in touch with her. I left my name and number and hung up. I was zero for two on the calls but at least I knew where Andorra Stevens and little Suzie weren't.

I ate breakfast at the Cadman Restaurant, which was a diner with a fancy name across the park from the Brooklyn federal courthouse. With a full stomach and my nerves wired with three cups of coffee, I was ready to spend the day tracking down the Stevens mother and daughter. My Boxster was parked on Orange Street and as I eased out of the space and headed down the street,

I could see through the side view mirror that a black Chevy Tahoe was pulling out behind me.

As I turned through the narrow streets, heading south towards Atlantic Avenue, the Tahoe stayed with me. The sun was bright and I had the top down, looking like an urbanite taking a leisurely morning jaunt. Until right before Atlantic when I slowed, watching the light change to yellow before I jammed my foot on the gas pedal. I made a sharp turn onto the avenue just as the light flicked red. That fixed the Tahoe, except that it sped through the red light and pulled up in traffic right behind me, making no effort to conceal that it was tailing me.

I gave up trying to lose it but when I parked across the street from the Brooklyn North headquarters, it was gone. Inside, I told the police aide sitting behind the Plexiglas divider that I wanted to see Lieutenant Lou Parella of the Auto Crimes Task Force. She checked the roster, picked up the phone and said a few words into it, then nodded and hung up. Sliding the visitors log towards me, she said someone would be down to escort me to Parella's office. I signed the log and waited.

When I looked inside the watch room, I could see Sergeant Ike Spaulding, Parella's right-hand man, standing at the foot of the stairs, an unlit cigar crammed underneath a thick mustache.

His heavy ebony face split into a grin when he saw me and he waved a sheaf of papers at me in a come on over motion.

"Counselor, what brings you to the Bat Cave?"

I told him I needed to see Parella on a personal matter.

"Personal matter," he repeated slowly, the grin still fixed on his face. "Right."

Ignoring the sarcasm, I asked, "Where is he?"

Spaulding motioned up the stairs where I knew the Brooklyn North Auto Crimes Task Force was located in a cramped set of back rooms. At the top of the stairs, I walked down the hall to the tiny office that had the name plate "LT L. Parella" tacked to the door. I knocked and opened the door just as Parella said, "Come in."

"Doherty, what brings you into the clutches of the NYPD on a lousy August day like this?"

The office was a small, beaten up room, one of a thousand used by law enforcement workhorses throughout the city. Parella had not even tried to liven it up, knowing it was a losing battle. Its smallness was made even more constrictive by a bank of battered putty-colored metal file cabinets that lined one wall. The only furniture was Parella's desk, a couple of wooden chairs and a small ratty couch covered with case files. A clothes tree stood sentinel in the far corner and the air conditioner rattled noisily. I took a seat in one of the chairs and explained in a vague way why I needed the NYPD's help.

"The Department resources are not at the disposal of the civilian population, you know that."

"I know, Lou, and I'm not asking you to violate Department rules, at least not major ones." I leaned forward, closer to him. "Remember the Lee Burke case?"

Parella nodded glumly and the tattooed eagle on his forearm started quivering. Lee Burke had been a contract killer but he botched a job and when I was still with the Brooklyn D.A.'s office, I prosecuted him for attempted murder. Parella was to have been my star witness.

"The judge said no more adjournments and sent me out to pick a jury. And you were supposed to go on vacation the next day, a scuba-diving trip to Bonaire. Your airline tickets and hotel were already booked and paid for, I believe?"

Parella nodded again.

"And the judge expected you testify the day after you were to leave. You would have eaten the airfare and hotel deposit and the Department would have had to pay you overtime."

"So what's your point?"

I leaned even closer to him. "The point is that right before jury selection, I paraded up and down the courtroom, vowing that if Burke was convicted, I would have the court declare him a mandatory persistent felony offender and demand a life sentence after conviction. I browbeat the defense attorney into having his client plead to the top count. And you got to go on your vacation, after all. And the Department saved on OT. It was a win-win situation for you. And now I need some help from the Department."

Parella leaned back in his chair and sighed. "What is it?"

I opened the manila folder and slid one of the photos of the Stevens girl over to him.

"Who's this?"

"Her name is Suzie Stevens. Her mother is Andorra Stevens and her father is Armstrong Stevens the Third."

Parella shrugged. "So he's got three sticks at the end of his name. I'm supposed to be impressed?"

"A good friend of the Mayor. A very good friend."

He arched his eyebrows.

"The girl is missing and I'm supposed to find her."

"Sounds like a job for Missing Persons or the FBI." His eyebrows were still arched.

"The Mayor and Stevens want this kept unofficial, out of the press."

"So they picked you?"

"You think I can't handle it?"

Parella grinned. "Oh, I know you can handle it, I just don't know whether to believe you."

"Would I kid you?"

He turned his head and tugged at an ear lobe. The eagle on his forearm was quivering again. He turned back and picked up the phone and punched in a number. "Hello, this is Lieutenant Parella of Brooklyn North Auto Crimes. Is the Mayor's secretary around? . . . Oh, this is she. I'm trying to get a hold of Armstrong Stevens, is he with the Mayor right now?" Parella cupped his hand over the receiver and listened and nodded. "Lunch on Friday, you say. Thank you."

Parella hung up the phone and smiled at me. "Doherty, you just may have picked a winner here."

"Why do I feel otherwise, then?" I said. "This seems an impossible task."

"Of course it is. Nobody could expect you to do the work of the Department or the FBI. Just go all out and turn in the best report you can. If the girl's still missing, her father will have to go to the authorities."

I wasn't so sure but I said, "So you'll help me, then?"

"Tell me what you need?"

I gave him the description of Andorra Stevens's Lexus and the license plate number. "Can you run this through the Department computer and see if there are any traffic violations or accident reports and check with the Parking Violations Bureau about tickets—and where and when?—Also, can you run a credit check on her?"

"You know this is a serious breach of Department policy, don't you?

"Lou, if I get the girl back, Stevens and the Mayor will know that it was with your help."

Parella laughed. "Yeah, that and two bucks will get me on the subway." He stood and offered me his hand. The eagle on his forearm was calm now. "I'll ask Ike to help out. Just make sure this stays between the three of us." He smiled a tired smile. "I guess it's not too much for a friend of the Department."

I smiled back and headed for the door. As I turned the knob, I stopped. "Do you still scuba?"

"Every chance I get. Which is not too often these days."

"When this is over with, we'll do a trip—on Stevens's money."

Parella waved me goodbye with a flick of his hand.

3

As I walked towards my car I was glad Lou Parella was willing to help, but I still felt uneasy. This case sure didn't seem like a winner despite Lou's pep talk. I couldn't put my finger on it, couldn't pin it down, but an ugly feeling had been lurking in my gut, right from the start, and when I drove away it was still with me. Whatever it was.

By the time I reached home I had stopped trying to figure it out but as I eased the Boxster into a parking space across the street from my apartment, Parella's words were whispering in my ears. No one expects you to do what the Department and the FBI can do. I knew he was right and that bothered me, too, made me wonder if Stevens was more concerned about bad publicity than his little girl's safety.

I was chewing this nasty thought over as I fumbled for the key to the building's front door. I was about to insert it into the lock when a large hand rested on my shoulder and a voice said, "Here, let me help you."

"No thanks," I said as I pivoted and launched a solid right towards the middle of whoever was behind me. My fist landed with a hard thud. That was it, nothing else. I stared up into the dull brown eyes of a large square face about four inches higher than mine and connected to a body maybe fifty pounds heavier. All muscle.

"That wasn't very nice, Mr. Doherty," the voice said.

I was about to send another right to his midsection when the door opened behind me and someone wrapped a hairy forearm around my throat and the odor of Sen Sen flooded into my nostrils. Suddenly, I was being dragged inside as the tall man followed.

"Let's go upstairs to your place, Mr. Doherty. Nice and easy so no one gets hurt."

I tried to reach for the tall man but the hairy arm tightened around my neck, cutting the blood flow. Red spots formed in front of my eyes and I twisted left, then right, trying to loosen the hold before the circulation cut off caused me to lose consciousness.

"Easy, Chiefy," the tall man said. "He's no good to us dead."

I felt myself being dragged further back inside towards the elevator. I was going under, smelling Sen Sen and watching the dancing red balls in front of me when suddenly the pressure eased.

"Are you going to give us any more trouble, Mr. Doherty?" the tall man asked.

I shook my head no.

Inside the elevator, they faced me towards the corner, Chiefy's forearm still wrapped across my throat. While the car rose, the tall man took the house keys out of my hand and patted me down.

"He's clean, you can ease up."

Chiefy spun me around to face the tall man.

"We're going into your apartment and have a little talk," the tall man said. "A friendly little talk. No one gets hurt as long as long as you cooperate. And you are going to cooperate, aren't you?"

I nodded my head.

When we reached my floor, Chiefy walked me to the end of the hall, his arm on my shoulder, real friendly like, the tall man with the square face following behind us. He handed the keys to Chiefy and said, "Open it and check the place out." Inside, the foyer was dark and Chiefy groped for the light switch. Suddenly he screamed and hopped on one leg. I rammed a shoulder into him, turned and kicked the tall man in the groin. He gasped but didn't fall, started to shake the pain off when I ducked inside and slammed the door.

Chiefy was still jiggling his leg and screaming when I punched him in the throat. He collapsed like a sack of rocks and lay on his side, gurgling. I took the keys out of his hand and frisked him quickly. The tall man was tapping gently on the door.

"It's okay, Mr. Doherty, we're not going to hurt you."

I ignored him and continued going through Chiefy's pockets. When I figured he was clean, I reached down and picked up Momma Sweet who was rubbing against my legs.

"Good girl," I said, petting the top of her head. "You scared the hell out of Chiefy here."

"Open the door, Mr. Doherty."

"No thanks, I'm not in the mood for company."

"Let Chiefy go then, we don't want trouble any more than you do."

"I like trouble. It breaks up the day."

"Don't be a wise guy, Mr. Doherty."

I set Momma Sweet down. "I'm calling the cops," I said.

"Don't be that way, we just want to talk."

I flipped on the foyer light. Chiefy was holding his throat, trying to sit up. Momma Sweet was hissing at him. I kicked Chiefy in the head and he keeled back over onto the floor. Momma Sweet seemed to like that.

"Talk about what?" I said through the door.

"Just let me in and I'll take Chiefy and leave."

"I'm calling the cops now."

"Let me in."

I didn't answer, just looked at Chiefy curled up on the parquet wood, out cold.

"Mr. Doherty?"

I stayed quiet, not moving.

"Let me speak to Chiefy," the tall man said.

"I'm afraid he's indisposed." I looked at the ugly purple welt on the unconscious man's forehead.

After a long moment. "Okay, I'm leaving but you're going to lose out on a big pay day."

"Pay day for what?" Despite my better sense, I had to ask.

"We want you to find someone. It's worth ten large. Five thousand in cash now, the rest on delivery." The tall man's voice was almost a whisper through the metal door.

"Who?"

"Andorra Stevens, the woman you're already looking for. But when you find her, you tell us instead of her husband."

"Why so much money?"

"Whaddya care? Don't be smart and ask too many questions. Just take the money and find the Stevens woman."

"I'm not looking for her; I'm looking for her daughter."

"Same thing. Find one, find the other," he said.

"Give me a number. I'll think about it and call you."

"I don't think so. I'm leaving an envelope with fifty c-notes outside your door. If you want the job, take the money. Otherwise, put it in Chiefy's pocket."

I didn't answer him.

After another long moment, he said, "I'm going now. Be smart and take the deal."

I waited fifteen minutes, then I cracked open the door and peered out. The hallway was deserted, only a lone fly was buzzing on a window pane. It was a helluva of an effort getting Chiefy downstairs and out of the building. I was exhausted but I managed to prop him up in a sitting position against the wall of the movie theatre on the corner, figuring a radio motor patrol from the eight-four would come by and toss him in the drunk tank.

By the time I parked the Boxster across the street from the Brooklyn North Auto Crimes office, I had calmed back down. In the police parking lot was the shiny black Chevy Tahoe. I couldn't see through the tinted windows so I had no idea whether it was occupied. But it didn't take me long to find out.

Lou Parella handed me a cup of coffee and led me back toward his office. It was completely different than just a few hours ago. The a/c unit was humming silently, pushing drafts of cold air towards me. Parella's desk was clean of paperwork, only a new blotter and the phone bank rested on its polished surface. Gone were the stacks of case folders on his couch and in their place sat a sandy-haired man in a dark suit. Lounging in a leather chair next to him was another man, sporting a shaved head and goatee, in a similar dark suit. His skull gleamed like Kojak's but his physique would put a professional wrestler to shame. He was the older of the two but he looked over at his sandy-haired companion, as if to take his cues from him.

It wouldn't be unusual for Parella to have a couple of detectives in his office to discuss ongoing cases, after all it was his job to supervise. But I knew that this pair, with their nondescript black suits and nondescript navy blue ties, were not NYPD.

"Ray Littlefield and Jim Bowman," Parella nodded at the man on the couch, then at the one in the leather chair. "They're with the Treasury Department."

"So this is the formal introduction?" I said. "It seems like we've already become friends, sort of."

Littlefield gave a short laugh. "I figured you would make our tail. I told Jim he should have let me drive; he likes to cowboy a bit too much. Hey, no harm done; actually we're glad to meet you face to face."

I sipped some of Parella's lousy coffee. "Why is that?"

"So we can tell you to stop looking for Andorra Stevens, you're interfering with a government investigation."

"You know where she is?"

"We have a pretty good idea." This came from Bowman. Littlefield threw him an annoyed look, then said, "We really would like you to back off."

"What if I don't?"

"That would be a very foolish decision on your part," he said. "There's a lot at stake here, much more than the penny ante fee you're earning. We don't need you stumbling around and screwing everything up."

I sat on the corner of Parella's desk and stared at Littlefield. "I've done a lot of very foolish things in my life, why should I stop now?"

"Because the nation's security may be at risk," Bowman said.

Littlefield shot him another annoying look.

"So tell me about it," I said.

Littlefield rubbed his chin. "Doherty, you keep this up, you're going to find yourself in serious trouble."

"What I'm finding is a cloud of smoke you're trying to blow up me." I turned to Parella. "Lou, did you bring these guys here to give me the okie-doke?"

He raised his hands palms up. "Not my doing. They just invited themselves in." He looked at Littlefield. "Doherty has always been a friend of the Department, he's not a troublemaker."

"Could have fooled me," Bowman said.

Littlefield rubbed his chin again and took a deep breath. "This is a classified matter but I can tell you this much, Armstrong Stevens owns a large hedge fund. Omega Global."

"I knew that."

He ignored my interjection and continued. "They invest in gold, copper, foreign currencies."

"I know that, too."

"Did you know that they also invest in strategic metals like titanium, molybdenum and uranium ore?"

I didn't know that, so I sipped my coffee and decided to keep my smart mouth shut.

"Stevens also owns a shipping company. Omega Global Freight Line and he's able to make off the radar bulk deliveries around the world."

I didn't know that, either, and it must have showed on my face.

Littlefield took a deep breath. "That's right. Most of his trading is away from the commercial exchanges and there's much room to disguise the transactions and hide income from taxation. Lots of income."

"What's this got to do with his wife and little girl?" I asked.

Littlefield took another deep breath and let it out slowly as if he was unsure how to continue. "We believe Andorra Stevens can give us information about her husband's hidden assets."

It was my turn to take a deep breath. "What makes you think that?"

"We've spoken to her about it."

I eased myself off the desk and stood in front of Littlefield. "When? Where is she? Is her daughter with her?"

"Easy, pard," Littlefield said. "We briefly interviewed her a few weeks ago. Then she took a powder."

"But you said you know where she is." I leaned towards his face.

"I said that we have a pretty good idea. If we had our hands on her, we wouldn't be talking to you. Now, back off."

I sat back on the edge of the desk and drank the rest of my coffee, grimacing at its sour taste and the even more sour news Littlefield was giving me.

"That bad, huh?" Bowman said.

"That bad."

"Hey, don't insult my coffee, it's free. You can always go to Starbucks."

"Sorry, Lou," I said. Turning back to Littlefield, "I was retained to work a case and that is to bring a little girl back to her father. I know where the mother isn't and you know where she might be, so why don't we join forces?"

Littlefield shook his head. "It's not that simple. Stevens has powerful friends in Washington. It would be bad enough if they learned we were investigating him, but that we somehow co-opted an attorney he retained on a legal matter ..." his voice trailed off, yet I caught his drift.

Bowman leaned forward. "We'd like to get the little girl as much as you do," he said.

Again, Littlefield shot him a glaring look. And I had figured out why. If the feds had little Suzie in their custody, they could secure Andorra Stevens' cooperation. What a great bunch.

"Is that why you sent those two goons to my apartment, to buy my assistance and to threaten me?"

"What goons?" Littlefield said.

"Yeah, Doherty, what goons?" Parella chimed in.

I ran down the story to them, how I was yoked in my doorway and forced upstairs by the tall man and Chiefy, and the struggle and the ten thousand dollar offer to find Andorra Stevens.

While I spoke, Bowman scribbled some notes and when I was done, Littlefield leaned back and spread his arms out along the couch. "You see what we mean, Doherty? It's a big league game and there are a lot of players. A broken down valise like you doesn't stand a chance on this trip."

"I seem to have done okay," I said.

"That's because those two jamokes had orders to talk to you, not clip you."

Littlefield had a point, I could see that. I looked at Parella. "Those two guys familiar to you?" I asked him.

He rubbed his eyes. "I'm afraid so." He let out a sigh. "A couple of small-time hoods from Brighton Beach, connected with Mo Vinogradov. I had them in here last year for questioning about an auto junkyard murder. Nothing on them, though. I can have my boys pick them up on attempted robbery charges if you want?"

"What? And help these guys out?" I jerked my thumb at Bowman. "Like the man said, they're a lot of players in the game, someone's bound to get lucky and find the Stevens woman."

"So you won't back off?" Littlefield said.

I shook my head. "I'm afraid not."

"Do this much for us, then, for your government, if you find Andorra Stevens, give us a call." Littlefield took a little leather folder out of his jacket pocket and handed me a business card.

I took it and turned it over in my hands. "I'll tell you what, if I get the little girl, I'll call you about her mother."

He grimaced. "Doherty, you know we could have you locked up."

"On what charge? Disturbing an investigation? I'd be out in a few hours and Armstrong Stevens would be raising hell with your bosses's bosses. And where would that leave you?"

Littlefield threw up his hands. "Have it your way, then. But don't come crying to us to pull you out of the manure pile when you start sinking."

I tossed my empty coffee container in the waste basket and left.

4

Armstrong Stevens's building was in a prime section of Park Avenue, its upper floors commanding sweeping views over the shorter, adjacent structures. Central Park to the west, the East River, of course, to the east. Bluebloods wouldn't have it any other way. The building had twenty-two floors and Stevens's duplex took up the nineteenth and twentieth. I had called ahead and the concierge was expecting me. After I signed in, I rode a teak paneled elevator up. There were only two units on the nineteenth floor and Stevens was on the right, which also gave him southern views of Manhattan, I guessed with Grand Central Station and the Chrysler Building nearby, the Empire State Building not too far beyond them.

I pressed the door buzzer and a petite olive-skinned woman in a domestic uniform answered.

"My name is Doherty. Mr. Stevens is expecting me," I told her.

"Adora, who is it?" a female voice sounded from somewhere inside.

Adora motioned for me to enter. "It is Mr. Doherty, for Mr. Stevens," she said.

"Bring him into the library, please."

I followed Adora into a large room with three walls lined with floor to ceiling bookcases. The fourth wall was adorned with a massive window that looked out over midtown Manhattan and the East River. I was right, Grand Central Station and the Chrysler Building loomed large on the skyline.

The furniture was a mix of colonial American and what I took to be Korean traditional. In a corner, near the large window was a partner's desk, which looked like an original Chippendale. Facing it was a hump-backed sofa, with some sort of toile fabric, also looking Chippendale. Seated on the sofa was a slim blonde with bobbed hair, wearing a mid-thigh clingy dress in swirling black, gray, white and off-white patterns, which made her look as if she was arising out of the sea.

"Thank you, Adora," she said. Standing up, she said to me, "I'm Janet Padavan. You must be the Mr. Doherty that's helping to find my darling little Suzie."

I nodded, saying nothing, too busy trying to figure out what she was doing here and what she meant by her "darling little Suzie." I walked over to the window and looked out.

"Magnificent view, don't you think?" It was more of a comment than a question.

I turned to look at Janet Padavan and instead found myself focusing on the bookcase opposite me. In a wide niche that split the structure in half, a gilded stone Buddha rested, surveying the room though contemplative eyes. Padavan followed my gaze and smiled.

"It's striking isn't it?" she said. "From the late Koryo Dynasty, I believe. One of Mrs. Stevens's prized possessions. Made of soapstone, it was lacquer-coated and then gilded."

I walked over to the niche. Below the golden Buddha was a *morijang* or chest to store socks and such. Early 14th Century, maybe the Yi Dynasty was my limited guess. On its top was a six-sided polished white stone brush holder with inlaid black color character designs, and a black marble ink stone with a folk scene of a scholar drinking under a plum tree. Next to the chest was a stone wash basin, maybe three feet high, also Yi. In front of another bookcase was a polished walnut vitrine. Through the glass top of the vitrine, I could see an aged and frayed Chinese character book, the kind that those privileged enough to become literate could use to practice calligraphy.

"A rather strange mix of furniture, it seems."

Padavan laughed. "I see you noticed. I wish I could say that all this is a product of an eclectic mind."

"Instead of?" I walked over to her and looked down into her eyes.

She looked up at me. "Instead of the unlikely aesthetic combination of an arranged blue-blood marriage. The colonial furniture is Mr. Stevens; this apartment was his before the marriage. The Korean objects were inherited by Mrs. Stevens from her father. He was a retired Army officer who had served in Korea. They form the basis of her collection, she's built a very expensive holding around them. Most of the more valuable pieces are on loan to museums; safer and no insurance premiums to pay."

"You said they had an arranged marriage."

She laughed again. "Perhaps I put it a little too crudely. I meant arranged in the manner that old money tends to marry old money, and the gene pool is always thinning."

"So the families knew each other?"

"Like two peas in a Swiss bank vault." She sat back down on the sofa and gestured to a spot next to her.

I sat down and draped one arm over the back. "Any reason Mrs. Stevens would pick up and leave?"

"None that I can think of." She smiled and crossed a pair of delicious looking legs.

"What about this teacher Suzie was supposed to testify against in the disciplinary hearing? Could he have abducted her and her mother?"

Janet laughed. "Dave Schmukler? He hasn't got the stones, if you pardon my Latin. No, I'm sure he has nothing to do with this."

I decided to come straight at her. "Why are you here?"

"This whole thing has been hard on Mr. Stevens. I thought I could help out." She saw the look on my face. "Oh, it's no bother, I just live across the park."

"Don't teachers go away for the summer? Travel, see the Louvre and the Coliseum, things like that?"

"I prefer New York when everyone's out of town. Besides, the Stevens are happy to have me continue tutoring Suzie. And they pay very well."

I looked down at the expensive wrist watch she was wearing. "And you can enjoy the finer things, of course."

"Of course." She smiled a dazzling smile.

I looked at my watch and took a deep breath. "I was supposed to brief Mr. Stevens."

"Oh, I am so sorry. He had to run out to a business meeting. Perhaps you can fill me in on the progress of your investigation."

It was my turn to smile. "I'm following some leads. Nothing solid but they may prove to pan out."

"That seems awfully vague, not much," she said.

She was right, it was vague, but I wasn't going to tell her about the feds' investigation into Stevens's business transactions and their interest in finding his wife. Hell, I wasn't even sure I was going to tell Stevens and he was my client. Sort of.

"I'm going to be busy for the next few days." I wrote out my cell number and gave it to her and asked her to tell Stevens to call me if he wanted an update. "I better get going now," I said, standing up.

Janet also stood. "Let me walk you to the door."

As we shook hands, she said, "I wish you all the luck. I'm sure you'll do a good job. We're counting on you." She smiled warmly, then closed the door.

There was a marina on the East River in Kips Bay and even though I had called the other day and spoke to the manager, I decided to drive down and scope the scene in person. It was a slow drive though the midday traffic and if Littlefield and Bowman were still tailing me, I didn't spot it or any other tick that might be on my back.

It was summer now and the fragrances wafting off the river weren't honeysuckle or bougainvillea. But, hey, to each his own. If this is what the marina club members wanted so they could show off their magnificent boats to the neighbors, more power to them. Inside, I offered the photo of little Suzie around but no one seemed to recognize her. I left a copy with the manager, my cell phone number scrawled on the back.

I had the list of yacht clubs I had googled and I decided to win-now it down, using my common sense. Andorra Stevens wouldn't go anywhere she would be recognized by social acquaintances. So I crossed off seven of the most exclusive clubs. She also wouldn't hide in someplace too downscale for her old money sensitivities. That removed almost thirty more from the list. I was left with a now workable list of thirteen yacht clubs and marinas. I started in Westchester, hitting Larchmont and Mamaroneck, then swinging back south, I crossed the Throgs Neck Bridge and canvassed the north shore of Long Island, starting with Port Washington, then Sea Cliff and Glen Cove, and worked my way east until I reached Cold Spring Harbor. A grizzled salt who was filling up a cutty cabin fishing boat thought he recognized Suzie, he had seen a girl who he said looked like her with a woman in her mid-thirties.

"There's a c-note waiting if you see her again," I said. He threw me a gap-toothed smile and said with a whiskey breath that he'd be on the lookout, I could count on him.

I hadn't eaten all day, so I drove down to Freeport for some seafood and a couple of beers, afterwards hitting a couple of more places on the south shore before calling it a day. Back home, I checked for messages with the service. Nothing. I went through the day's mail, which consisted of bills and solicitations to spend more of the money I didn't have. I fed Momma Sweet and Diva, took a hot shower, poured myself a stiff JD on the rocks and hit the bed. Even with the booze to numb me, I couldn't fall asleep. I kept wondering why Shanahan picked me for this case and what did he know, if anything, about the U.S. Treasury's investigation of Stevens, the Mayor's great pal. Just to make sure I stayed awake, I interspersed these worries with visions of Janet Padavan's luscious legs parading before me.

5

The next morning Momma Sweet and Diva awoke me after about thirty minutes of sleep. My head ached from fatigue and a debate raged inside whether to make some coffee or pour another JD. I decided to be good for a change and opted for the coffee.

When I left the apartment I made sure that the tall guy and Chiefy weren't around. Everything looked clear so I stepped outside and walked to my Boxster. It was already hot, the weather man said low nineties with high humidity and possible thunderstorms. I wasn't excited about continuing my canvass so I called my service to see if anything else was up. One message, a number only.

"Doherty?" said a gruff voice when I called back. "Elmer Long. You remember me?"

"Sure. The marina worker in Cold Spring Harbor," I said.

"Still lookin' for that little girl?"

"Have you seen her?"

"Are you still offering a c-note?"

"What can you tell me?"

"Can you make it more than a hundred? I got a kid in law school."

"If it's good, two bills."

"Deal," he cackled. "Well, you know I also work in Huntington Harbor so I'm down there a lot and I got to talking about this little girl. Someone said they had seen a girl just like her steering a sailboat. I said I didn't believe him, bet him ten dollars he couldn't show me the boat. Got a pen?"

I wrote down the name of the marina and the description of the boat.

My shirt was soaked through and beads of sweat from my forehead rolled down under my sunglasses and stung my eyes. I needed to call Stevens and get him out here to take custody of the kid and swore when I realized that I had left the manila folder with his private number scrawled on it back at the apartment. So I was in no mood to enjoy the fresh salt air when I punched the number into the cell phone. After six rings, Adora answered.

"This is Doherty. I need to speak to Mr. Stevens."

She told me to wait. A few moments later Janet Padavan picked up the receiver. "Mr. Doherty? Mr. Stevens will be back in a half-hour. Do you have any news?"

"Tell him," I said, "that I found Suzie."

"What? Where is she? I can't believe it. You are so wonderful."

"Whoa, slow down." I gave her the address of the marina in Huntington Harbor and the description of the boat. "That's right, a 57-foot Beneteau. Stevens can't miss it; I'll wait at the end of the dock for him."

"Is she okay?"

"I'm watching the boat now." As I was speaking, Andorra Stevens came topside and started checking the stays. They were getting ready to sail. "Just tell Stevens to get here now." I hung up and crouched behind a wooden trash bin. The heat was oppressive and the spot was cramped and I didn't want to talk with Janet any more than I had to. I just wanted this job to end with my client happy and nobody hurt.

I should have known better.

I was positioned in my observation post so the sun beat down on my neck and back. It was better than in my face but not much better. My legs were cramping up but I couldn't stand and stretch. It was too risky, Andorra Stevens might spot me. Besides, she might not be alone. I looked at my watch. Forty minutes had passed. Stevens should be here soon. I wiped my eyes, the salty sweat was stinging the corners and forcing me to squint.

A radio crackled and I could hear a female voice. Andorra Stevens. She was a doing a five-by-five, the radio check to make sure that it was working properly before they shoved off. I couldn't wait any longer for Stevens, I had to make my move now. I scuttled along the dock until I reached the short wooden gangway that led to the Beneteau. Easing up the gangway, I dropped down into a wide on-deck dining area. I hid behind a table, scrunched up under the large steering wheel. If Stevens didn't get here fast, my options would be only one. When Andorra Stevens and little Suzie came up on deck to cast off, I would grab the girl and run.

The radio was crackling again, raspy noises filtering up through the hatch sounded like a Coast Guard weather report.

Here in the boat, the sun was directly in my face and I had to keep wiping the sweat away, but every so often a breeze came in off the water, making my surveillance tolerable if not pleasurable. I had to stay where I was, it didn't make sense to go down the hatchway and confront them. Anyone sailing a boat this expensive would keep a firearm on board. Hell, maybe more than one.

Fifteen minutes later, I knew I was right. There was a firearm on board. A pistol. And the barrel was jammed in the back of my neck.

"Stay where you are," Janet Padavan said. "I know you're unarmed, I checked the cut of your jacket yesterday at the duplex. So I won't shoot unless you do something stupid."

"But that's my best act," I said. "Besides, you won't shoot me here, out in the open. The noise will carry over the water."

Janet gave a short laugh. "That's why I've got a suppressor. It'll sound just like another champagne cork popping. Except your blood will be flowing, not fine bubbling wine—from a nice neat hole in the base of your skull—so let's go down the hatchway and see who's home." She prodded me with the gun.

As we edged down the hatchway steps I could hear the radio still crackling and a female voice speaking softly. When we reached the bottom step I found myself looking into a stateroom with long couches on both sides. The fabric covering them was expensive and plush striped pillows adorned the seating surfaces. Suzie Stevens was at a table in front of one of the couches, drinking a soda. I didn't see her mother.

Janet Padavan pushed me forward with her pistol and Suzie looked up.

"Ms. Padavan." Suzie stood and started toward us but froze when she saw the pistol jammed in the nape of my neck. Suddenly, her mother appeared from the side of the room and grabbed her.

"You," she said to Janet. "What are you doing here? Haven't you done enough to my family? And who's he?"

"My name's Doherty. Your husband retained me to find Suzie."

Janet waved the barrel of the gun at Andorra Stevens. "Now I know why I dislike you. You talk too much. So take your little brat and sit down on the couch over there and shut up."

Andorra Stevens glared at her. "I thought you were our friend. We bring you into our home and you steal my husband—and now this?"

Janet flashed her set of perfect white teeth. "You're married to a billionaire in waiting, you live on Park Avenue, have a *cottage* in Newport. I spend my days in a classroom filled with snotty-nosed kids and have to tutor little brats for some extra scratch. Friends? We could never be friends."

"So you take my husband and destroy our marriage?"

"Take your husband?" Janet laughed. "Is that what you think? You really are a stupid cow." She waved the pistol at Andorra Stevens. "I told you to sit down."

When the woman and her daughter sat, Padavan looked around. "You live better here, on this boat, than I could ever hope to live as a teacher." She prodded me with the gun. "Go over there and stand by them, Doherty."

I walked over to where Suzie sat and let my hand rest on the table, near the glass of soda. I could see Janet was holding a Smith & Wesson automatic in her hand, and she seemed comfortable with it.

She still had a smile on her face as she faced Andorra Stevens. "Your husband is all business. Sure he was attracted to me, we had a few laughs, but he loves you—though I don't know why—and his hedge fund. So I'll just have to settle for what you brought with you."

I didn't know what she was talking about and Janet could see the bewilderment on my face. "Doherty, are you really that stupid, too?" she said.

Here I was, unarmed, facing a loaded automatic, with no plan, and a great likelihood that I'd never get to spend the retainer for this case. Yeah, I guess I really was that stupid.

"Where is it?" she asked Andorra Stevens.

Andorra said nothing.

"Where is what?" I said.

"My gawd, Doherty, haven't you figured it out?"

"No, was I supposed to?" I was feeling tired, worried, maybe even scared.

"Well, let me clue you in. Blueblood bimbo over here figured her husband was having an affair with me."

"But you weren't," I said.

"Oh my god," Andorra Stevens gasped.

I still didn't get it.

"So she took off with Suzie—and some insurance. A little notebook with her husband's numbered bank accounts in Liechtenstein and the Cayman Islands. And dates and amounts of transactions." She smiled at Andorra Stevens. "I guess you figured that as long as you had the evidence of him hiding his income, he wouldn't contest custody of your precious little darling."

Andorra Stevens's hand flew to her mouth. "How could I have been so stupid?" Her voice was almost a whisper.

"That's supposed to be my line," I said. I turned to Janet. "What I don't understand is how you knew about the little book."

"I overheard Armstrong talking on the phone to his attorney. He said the book was missing. It made sense Andorra took it."

"That must be why Stevens never went to the FBI or the police. He wanted the book back and if the authorities found it, it would cost him—what—millions?"

"Your light bulb has finally switched on, Mr. Doherty." Janet laughed. "Dim to be sure, but at least it's on now."

"And you suggested a very discreet, private inquiry, one you could keep track of."

"I thought that was a good touch."

"So Stevens goes to the Mayor who sends him to Shanahan who picks me."

"Somebody had to be the stooge." She was grinning at me. "The only question is whether you want to be a dead stooge?"

I shook my head. "So you had those two goons, the tall man and Chiefy encourage me to work a little harder—and to make sure Stevens didn't get his little book back."

"Another nice touch, don't you think? I got a hold of Mo Vinogradov, we grew up together in the old neighborhood, and I asked him for a favor, to offer you twenty-five thousand to work the case for him."

"Twenty-five? They only offered me ten large."

Janet laughed loudly. "Isn't that just like Mo, grabbing a major piece of the action for himself."

"Except it was really small potatoes, wasn't it? What were you going to do with the little book?"

"Shut up," Janet said to me. She waved the pistol at Andorra Stevens. "Now where is it? Can't remember? Maybe if little Suzie gets hurt ..."

Andorra cut her off. "No, I'll get it." She started to move off the couch.

Janet waved the pistol at her. "Take it slow." She walked over to Suzie and grabbed her. "Any tricks and I'll hurt little precious."

"Mommy." Suzie started to struggle.

Janet looked down at her and at the same time I scooped up the glass of soda and threw it in Janet's face. She screamed as the carbonated liquid hit her eyes and let go of Suzie, her free hand reflexively trying to wipe the liquid away. Regaining her vision, she swung her gun hand towards me. Just a little too late. I chopped the side of her neck with the blade of my hand and she sank to the floor like a sack of rocks. I knelt over her and took the auto out of her hand.

"Is she dead?" Andorra Stevens asked.

"No, but she'll be harmless for at least half an hour."

"What should I do, Mr. Doherty?"

I worked the action on the auto and a shell ejected. Janet Padavan had meant business.

"We've got to get out of here. She may not be alone."

"Are we still in danger?" She was hugging Suzie.

"I'm afraid so." I took a deep breath and exhaled slowly, trying to think this through. "I'll go to my car and get it started. If the coast is clear, I'll signal for you to come running with Suzie. Stay on deck until then."

Andorra Stevens nodded and squeezed Suzie's hand.

Outside, the sun beat down through a hazy blue sky. A lone gull sat on one of the pilings. The dock was deserted and when I reached the Boxster, I keyed the engine and eased the car over closer to the boat. I couldn't see anyone so I stuck my arm out the window and waved to Andorra.

They came down the gangway, Suzie breaking into a run towards my car. I opened the side door and she hopped in. Her mother was about twenty feet from us when the boom of a large caliber pistol erupted from somewhere behind me and the left side view mirror shattered.

I turned to see a dark-haired, heavy set figure in a gray sweatshirt moving by the bow of a dry-docked boat. He lifted a pistol and aimed it my way, the shot spidering the windshield just above my ducking head. I pushed Suzie down onto the floor, spun and snapped off two quick rounds. The man clutched his shoulder and fell forward, sprawling on the ground.

"Stay down and don't move," I told the girl. Getting out of the car, I rushed over to the fallen gunman and kicked his weapon away. Kneeling next to him, I could see it was Chiefy and that he still had a pulse. Running back to the car, I got in and yelled, "Andorra, let's go."

I was shifting the gear into drive when a shadow loomed at my side and another shot went off, the round burning across my forearm.

"Hold it right there, Mr. Doherty." It was the tall man. He opened the passenger side door and slid in, his feet shoving Suzie to the side.

"You've turned out to be a real pain in the butt," he said, his automatic pointed down at Suzie's head. "Where's Janet Padavan?"

I shrugged. "Relaxing in the boat, I guess. What brings you out here? Going fishing?"

"You're a funny man, Mr. Doherty." He reached over and patted me, found Janet's automatic stuffed between my thighs, and threw it out the passenger side window.

"Chiefy didn't think so."

"Yeah, well that's his problem. Now, Padavan has something Mo wants, something worth a lot of money. And you're going to help me get it. Or I kill the little girl here, then you, then her mother, and Janet, if I have to. So are you going to cooperate?"

His eyes were wide and his voice raspy, pumped up with the recent gunplay, and excited for more. So I took him at his word and nodded agreement.

"Okay, let's go to the boat. I get out first." The tall man reached for the door handle, his eyes still on me. He pushed the handle down, and then suddenly the lone sea gull flew off the filing and his eyes darted to the side.

I made my move, the only move I had left, grabbing his gun hand with both of mine, slamming it against the steering wheel. He was still holding the weapon and I slammed his hand again. He started punching my face with his free hand and even though he was punching at an awkward angle, the force of the blows rocked my head. But no matter how much it hurt, I knew I couldn't let go of the other wrist. I kept holding on but I was getting weaker from the punches and from the gunshot. I twisted his wrist, taking a left on my jaw, stunning me. He was strong, as strong as I was, and he just kept whaling away at my face. Because of the close quarters he still couldn't get a clear shot and that gave me a glimmer of hope. Still, the punches were effective and I was only holding onto the wrist of his gun hand now, no longer trying to free the weapon from his grasp. Another left pounded my ear, the concussion stunning me again. I was going under, knew it would soon be all over, when there was a crack of a gunshot and the tall man's head snapped back and sank limply like a rag doll's.

Through the blood and pain I could see the figure of Andorra Stevens standing outside the passenger's window. She was holding Chiefy's gun.

"Where's Suzie?" she screamed.

I pointed at the floor.

She opened the door and pushed the tall man's legs to the side and hugged the little girl.

"Put the gun down," I said, hearing a dreamlike quality in my voice.

She looked at me, then set the pistol in my lap.

I didn't touch it, just closed my eyes and listened to a loud humming in my ears. The humming was mixed with tinny piano-like noises. I opened my eyes again. Andorra was speaking to me, holding her hand out. I strained to understand what she was saying, tried to focus on her hand, what it was holding.

"What should I do with the notebook?" she asked.

I jerked my head toward the dock and the harbor beyond.

She walked over to the edge of the dock and flung the little book out onto the water. I saw tiny bubbles as it disappeared below the surface. Then I closed my eyes and listened as the humming in my ears turned to a whine and the piercing screams of sirens.

It was five p.m. and Lou Parella and I were seated in the emergency room at Huntington Hospital. Lou was sipping a hot cup of coffee while I was having my left arm bandaged where the bullet had grazed it. An intern was picking bits of glass out of my scalp, causing me to wince.

"Can't you even sit still when a pretty young thing is ministering to you?"

The young intern smiled. So did I. It was a moment of weakness.

"Mrs. Stevens has good aim," Parella said.

"She does."

"And you have good luck."

"I do."

"Nine millimeters cause lots of damage at close range. You have really good luck. What the hell happened?"

"It's a long story, Lou."

"Well, Suffolk County Homicide wants to hear it."

"How did you get out here?" I said.

He laughed. "Mo Vinogradov has been causing a lot of problems for Brooklyn North Auto Crimes. On a hunch, I had my boys tail those two jamokes. They radioed me when they spotted your Boxster. I told them to sit tight. Then the gunplay started. You know, everywhere you go, blood seems to spill."

"Yeah, yeah, I'm just a social pariah." I looked around. "Is the little girl okay?"

"Suzie? Ike took her down to the cafeteria for some ice cream."

I winced again as the intern applied some antiseptic. "What do you know about this?" I asked Parella.

"My guys were about to rush your car when Mrs. Stevens pops up and blows half of the tall man's head off."

"Where is she?"

"With the Homicide boys. When they let her go, Littlefield and Bowman want to take a crack at her."

"She doesn't know anything," I said.

Parella threw me a fish eye.

"She's a tough cookie," I said, changing the subject. "She and her daughter sailed the yacht down from Newport by themselves. Besides, the feds have nothing to hold her on. She's not her husband."

Parella shrugged. "Too bad for them that Stevens didn't leave a paper trail."

"Yeah, too bad." Stevens would never know it, though, that his little notebook with all the incriminating evidence was a soggy mass of paper and ink blobs at the bottom of the harbor. As far he knew, Andorra had stashed it somewhere for safekeeping and I was sure that she would never disabuse him of that notion.

And he would stay married to her. To his bitter half.

✗

A SHORT, SHARP, SHOCK

by Melville S. Brown

The woman stood on the corner of Edgeware Road and waved frantically for a taxi. There was an astonishing amount of traffic for a Sunday morning, but that was London in July. The weather was actually warm and sunny, and it seemed as if half the planet had come for a visit. She leaned out and was nearly sideswiped by a bus turning the corner.

Eventually a cab pulled up, and the woman jumped in, carrying a large satchel with papers sticking out of it. "Thirteen, Beaufort Place, please, and hurry!" she called out to the driver.

The cab drove south past the Marble Arch, with the driver, a Pakistani, weaving from one lane to another as best he could. He glanced in the rearview mirror at his passenger, who looked anxiously out the window. She was a young Englishwoman with short, dark hair, dressed in a navy blue suit.

"Working so early on a Sunday, Miss?" the driver said.

"Yes, I'm an estate agent. I have to get ready to show a flat to some clients." She glanced at her watch nervously, then stared out the window some more.

A few blocks later the woman's cell phone rang. "No, Simon, I won't be home for several hours," the driver heard her say. "I told you last night, remember? This showing will take me most of the day."

She rang off and the driver looked at her again. She put down her phone and leaned back to stare out the window.

"Well, it's a lovely day, Miss!" he said. The woman didn't answer. She just looked forlornly out the window, yawning conspicuously. The driver took his cue and didn't say anything more. He knew the English and their signals.

The driver raced past Hyde Park and finally stopped at a red light. Crowds of tourists passed in front of the taxi on their way to Buckingham Palace, where they could hang around hoping for a glimpse of a royal, or have their photo taken with a Beefeater.

Confused by the lights and traffic, they looked in both directions, inched forwards and backwards, then bravely shoved on. The driver honked impatiently when the light changed, and roared off at breakneck speed.

He pulled up in front of the house in record time, stopped the meter, and turned around. "That'll be seven pounds, fifty, Miss."

The woman stared out the window, mouth agape. She didn't move.

Detective Inspector Septimus Bracegirdle, wearing his best summer suit and tweaking his mustache, looked at the scene with dismay. It was a damned inconvenient time for a murder. He had been on a leisurely walk to St. Paul's Cathedral for the ten o'clock service when his Blackberry went off. Scotland Yard had ordered him over to South Kensington, miles away from Sir Christopher Wren's masterpiece, and he would never get back in time. Who knew when the Byrd Mass in Five Voices would be performed again, in such heavenly acoustics?

The woman's body had been pulled from the taxi she'd arrived in, and two emergency workers were frantically giving her artificial respiration. The driver, another refugee from the Jewel in the Crown, was shrieking to two young policemen that he knew nothing, that the passenger was fine when he picked her up.

"I tell you, she was okay!" he protested. "I drove really fast, like she asked me! We got here, I turned around, and she is dead. I never touch her!"

The two policemen, one a chubby blond kid, the other dark and athletic, looked at him skeptically. "Cool off a bit, mate," the blond one said to the driver.

"I say, who is this woman, does anyone know yet?" Bracegirdle said to no one in particular.

The handsome, dark kid came over. "Margaret St. Clair is her name. The driver says she was selling flats here." He scratched his head. "Probably makes a bloody fortune."

"Made," corrected Bracegirdle.

"Right. Well, Paki here says she wasn't up for a chat. They exchanged a few words, she talked to her husband on her cell, and that's it. Heart attack, if you ask me." He shrugged.

Bracegirdle looked back at the EMTs working on the body. They had torn her clothes open and were pounding her chest like bread dough. *God save me from being rescued*, thought the detective, as they blew air into her and pummeled her breasts.

He glanced into the cab and saw a cell phone on the floor. He put on gloves, then reached down and picked up the phone, holding it carefully in his palm. As he was looking it over, the EMTs put the woman into an ambulance with an oxygen mask. One of them, a tall fellow with flushed cheeks, came over to him.

"I think we got her back," he said. "But we won't know until she wakes up."

Bracegirdle raised his eyebrows. "She was still alive when you got here, then?"

"We didn't think so at first, because she was completely still and not breathing. But there was a pulse, so we went to work straight away."

"Not a heart attack, then?"

"No. A stroke, possibly."

"Awfully young for a stroke, don't you think?" Bracegirdle smiled and twisted his mustache. The EMT looked miffed and walked away.

Bracegirdle studied her phone. It was badly scratched, and a tiny splinter of metal casing stuck out just below the screen. The splinter was slightly stained.

"Just a minute," Bracegirdle said, and jumped into the ambulance. He looked at the woman's face under the oxygen mask closely. Just below her left ear was a small scratch which had begun to heal. He got out and went over to the driver, a slight, dark-skinned man in wrinkled, loose-fitting, Indian clothing, who was nervously smoking a cigarette.

"Tell me, young man, who did your passenger talk to on her cell phone?" Bracegirdle asked.

"I don't know. Someone named Simon." The driver stubbed out his cigarette. "I think her husband."

"Did she ring him, or did he make the call?"

"He rang her. It was very short, she didn't want to talk much."

"And do you remember anything she said?"

"Just that she'd be busy all day. She was a little angry because she had to remind him."

Bracegirdle took out his Blackberry and called Scotland Yard. "Septimus here." Everyone knew him by his first name. "Look, can you find out anything about a Margaret St. Clair for me? Also, her husband if you can. Yes, call me back as soon as you know."

He took a plastic bag from the ambulance supplies and put the woman's cell phone in it. Then he told the EMT to get a blood sample immediately.

His smartphone rang. "Morning, Septimus, this is Tom Fishburne," said the policeman on the other end. "St. Clair is an estate agent with Withers Properties, Ltd. Her husband is Simon St. Clair, a professor of Ethnology."

"Hello, Tom, thanks much. Any other info on the husband?"

"He has a specialty in Amazonian Indian tribal culture."

Bracegirdle cleared his throat. "Right. Send someone round immediately to arrest Professor St. Clair on suspicion of attempted murder. His wife appears to have been poisoned with curare!"

Bracegirdle rang off and went around to the sit next to the ambulance driver. As they tore off down the street, the EMT in the back yelled, "How was she poisoned?"

"Her husband bent off a sharp piece of the casing on her cell phone and dipped it in curare. Then he called her during the cab ride to make sure she used it and scratched herself with the poisoned tip." Bracegirdle toyed with his mustache. "Curare paralyzes the lungs immediately, but the victim remains alive for a time, unable to speak or breathe. Time is of the essence in these cases, so the driver probably saved her life by speeding. I say, talking of speeding, can you drop me off near St. Paul's? I'm late for the ten o'clock."

✗

THE MAN IN THE OVERCOAT

by Marc Bilgrey

Bob Wilson looked out the window of his west side apartment and watched the last traces of sunlight fade over the Hudson River. Then he turned and looked over at his wife, Linda. She was sitting on a chair across from him, reading a copy of *People* magazine. Only she wasn't reading it, he concluded, she was only pretending to read it. And every few seconds she would look up and stare off into space. What was that all about? Bob wondered, as he hid behind his copy of the *Times*. Then the phone rang.

"I'll get it," said Linda. Bob watched her walk to the phone and pick up the receiver. "Hello," she said. "Oh, hi Joyce. Yes, uh huh, sure, that sounds fine. See you then. Bye." She hung up the receiver and walked back to her chair and sat down. "That was Joyce," she announced (as if there were some doubt), "she wants to meet me now."

"Oh?" said Bob, trying to sound as casual as he could.

"Yes," said Linda. "Ken's out of town again and she's lonely. It must be hard to be the wife of a traveling salesman."

"This is the third time this month that he's been away," said Bob.

"I feel sorry for Joyce," said Linda. "I really do. You don't mind if I go over and see her, do you? I told her that I'd stop by."

"Well . . ." said Bob, placing his newspaper on the table under his reading lamp.

"Oh, be a dear."

"Doesn't she have any other friends?"

"Nobody that she can talk to," said Linda.

"I guess it'd be okay, but don't stay out too late. I worry about you."

"No reason to worry, all we do is sit around, drink tea and talk. Sometimes we play cards."

"I just don't like you walking around the city late at night."

"I'll try to get back early."

"Okay," said Bob. He watched Linda get up and walk to the hall closet.

"Joyce is such a nice woman," said Linda, as she opened the closet and took out her coat.

"It sounds like her husband doesn't treat her very well," said Bob.

"Oh, he's not a bad person. He's just never there for her," she said, as she put on her coat and buttoned it.

"I'd love to meet Joyce sometime," said Bob.

"Oh, you will," said Linda. "But she's really going through a lousy time right now, what with her thinking about getting a divorce and her mother being sick and all."

"Divorce is a big step."

"I know, that's what she's always talking to me about. Actually, I think she's a little envious of our marriage."

"Hmmmm," said Bob.

"I'll see you later, dear," said Linda, and kissed him on the cheek.

As soon as she was gone, Bob ran to his workroom, took a gun from inside a drawer, threw on a jacket and hat, locked the door and ran down the service stairs.

He arrived on the street just in time to see Linda get into a cab. He flagged down another cab and had the driver follow the first one. As Bob watched the taxi in front of him, he thought about the events leading up to all this. The day, four months ago, when Linda had told him that she'd met a woman at the supermarket named Joyce. After that, she and Joyce began talking on the phone constantly. Then there'd been the first time she'd said she was going over to her new friend's apartment to visit. There had also been the reported conversations about Joyce's husband, who was always on the road, and the thoughts that Joyce had had about divorcing him. Bob didn't believe a word of it.

The cab in front of him turned and headed east. Initially, Bob *had* believed all of it. And why not? It'd sounded very credible. A lonely woman wanting company when her husband was away. The bad marriage. The long talks. But over the weeks that followed, the story started developing little holes. Why, for instance, did Linda always go over to Joyce's, yet Joyce never visited Linda? Why did the visits become more frequent? And what about Linda's moods?

She'd often come back from a visit to Joyce, (one where Joyce had talked about her bad marriage), yet, Linda would seem happier than when she'd left. There were other things, little things that only a husband would notice. Like the laundry. The towels were folded differently, one crease instead of two. After fifteen years of marriage, why the change?

Bob put his hand in his pocket and felt the cold metal of the gun. In his heart he knew that there was no Joyce, but still, he decided, he would love to be proved wrong. He would love to see Joyce and then—but there was no Joyce and he knew it.

Linda's cab stopped in front of a hotel. She got out and went inside the building.

Bob paid his driver and scurried into the lobby after her.

The hotel lobby had a couple of dozen people milling around. Bob was pleased about that, figuring that the activity would give him a good cover and make him stand out less. Bob pulled his hat over his face and watched Linda walk to the far end of the lobby and into the gift shop. Bob looked around and decided that the hotel had probably once been beautiful. But now the carpets were a bit worn and the walls needed new paint. He couldn't help thinking that the place reminded him of his marriage.

Bob looked back at the gift shop and saw Linda flipping through a magazine. He scanned the crowd in the lobby, trying to spot who she was meeting. He saw a mix of foreign tourists, women with pink pant suits from the Midwest and flight attendants pulling suitcases on wheels.

Bob wondered what had driven Linda to this point. Was it the fact that he hadn't gotten his much anticipated promotion at work? He'd been passed over in favor of someone in another department. It wasn't Bob's fault that "the someone" turned out to be the boss' nephew. Bob wondered if maybe being in the office supply business wasn't glamorous enough for Linda. He'd often thought of doing something else. Or maybe it was just that he should have taken her out more.

Bob snapped out of his daze as a burly looking man in a hat and overcoat walked into the gift shop. As soon as he stepped inside the small store, Linda looked up from her magazine and smiled. She put the magazine back on the rack, and then she and the man walked out of the store toward the elevator.

So, thought Bob, this was who she'd been seeing for the last four months. This man was "Joyce."

Bob watched Linda exchange smiles with the man and then the elevator doors opened and they both stepped inside. A few other people also walked in. As soon as the doors closed, Bob went over to the elevator and looked at the indicator above it to see which floors it was stopping at. It stopped at four, nine, twelve and fifteen. He debated with himself what to do next.

Should he go upstairs and search for their room? There were an awful lot of rooms on the fourth, ninth, twelfth and fifteenth floors. Still, if he knocked on every door, he might eventually be able to find his wife and her lover. His wife and her lover! It was the first time he had actually thought those words. He didn't like the sound of them.

He decided there must be a more practical idea than running around the whole hotel on a wild goose chase. The solution was simple. He'd just wait till they were finished and then, when they left, he'd follow the man in the overcoat.

Bob went to the gift shop and bought a newspaper. Then he found a chair that allowed him an unobstructed view of the hotel's two elevators. He sat down and opened the paper. As he looked at an article he thought about his wife and her lover upstairs. The words on the page in front of him seemed meaningless, the letters, no more than little black marks.

Two hours later, the elevator doors opened and Linda and the man in the overcoat walked out. Bob covered his face with the newspaper. Through a pinhole, he watched his wife kiss the man and then the two of them walked out of the lobby. He ran after them.

Outside, the man in the overcoat placed Linda in a cab and then started walking downtown. Bob followed him. Half a block later, Bob reached into his pocket and felt his gun. Just touching it made him feel better.

Bob wondered how he would kill him. He didn't want any witnesses, and he certainly didn't want to get caught. Even though he thought it would be justifiable homicide, somehow, he didn't think that the police would agree. There was nothing to worry about, he told himself. He would follow this man and then, when everything looked safe, he would let him have it. And afterwards, everything would be okay. He would go home and that would be the end of it.

The man continued downtown on the dark streets. Bob wondered if he should approach him and talk to him. Then it occurred to him that maybe Linda had shown the man a picture of him, then he'd suspect that there was a problem. No, it was too risky. He wanted to surprise him, pounce on him, and then do the deed. No use warning the son of a bitch what was in store for him.

Twenty blocks later, the man was still walking. Where was he going? Bob asked himself. Then the man turned and went down a side street. Ah, thought Bob, progress. A block later, the man looked at his watch, stopped and leaned against a building. Bob wondered if he should shoot him right there. Suppose he did and then someone grabbed him and held him down till the police came? Or worse, suppose a cop just happened to be walking by.

Or a couple of them pulled up in a patrol car. No, he decided, he'd wait for the right moment, then do it.

Bob stood a half a block away and watched the man in the overcoat lean against the building. Every so often the man would glance at his watch. Half an hour went by, then an hour. What was he waiting for, wondered Bob. Bob noticed that the street was now very quiet. No car passed, a lone pedestrian hurried by and then was gone. Now would be the time, thought Bob. Now would be the time to kill him.

Bob reached into his pocket and took out the gun. He slowly walked forward. He decided that he would thrust the gun into the man's stomach and fire it. Then he wondered if he should say something first. Maybe something dramatic, like, "This is for Linda." It was too corny, he decided. Besides, it had to be done quickly, and talk would just slow the whole thing down. Just do the job, then get away as fast as possible, he told himself.

Bob walked toward the man in the overcoat. The gun was at his side, shielded by his jacket and the darkness. He felt his heart begin to pound. He'd never killed anyone before and the thought of doing it now did not give him any pleasure. His right hand began to shake. He steadied it. Everything would be over in just a few seconds, he told himself, and then order would be restored to the world again.

Bob was only a few feet from the man now. He gripped the gun handle tightly and was just starting to bring the weapon up, away from his own body, when suddenly somebody walked out of the building. Bob froze, his arm dropped back to his side.

The man in the overcoat turned and followed the man who'd just left the building.

The new man was wearing a dark suit and was bald. The man in the overcoat caught up with him, then loudly called out to him, "Belson?"

The bald man turned and faced the man in the overcoat. "Yeah?" he said.

Then the man in the overcoat pulled out a gun and shot him. Belson screamed and fell to the ground. The man in the overcoat looked at him for a few seconds, then calmly walked down the street.

Bob didn't move. He stared at the man on the sidewalk. Then, a few seconds later, he put the gun back into his pocket. He realized that he was so stunned that he didn't know what to do. Should he follow the man in the overcoat? Before he could make a decision, he became aware of a crowd of people standing behind him.

"I saw the whole thing," said a man. "This city's going to hell," said another. "Call an ambulance," said a third.

Somebody kneeled down next to the man on the sidewalk and said, "It's a little late for an ambulance."

A man who stood next to Bob said "The guy who did this is someone you don't want to mess with. That was Joey, Jr."

"Y-you know him?" asked Bob.

"Well, I don't know him personally," said the man, "but everyone knows Joey. Where you been living, in a cave? He's on the news all the time. He's the head of organized crime in this town. Last year, he personally killed at least ten people. Who knows how many other hits he's ordered that his men have carried out? The Feds can't seem to stop him. But hey, I didn't see nothing, if you get my drift. I got no idea who shot this poor bastard." Then the man frowned and walked away.

Bob took another look at the dead man, then pushed through the crowd and went to the comer. An ambulance and a police car were just driving up. Bob walked another block, found a cab and went home.

Bob walked into his apartment, took off his jacket and hung it up in the closet.

"Hi honey," said Linda, who was sitting on the couch.

"Hi," said Bob, with no enthusiasm, as he walked into the living room. "Where you been?" said Linda.

"Uh, I just went out to take a walk," said Bob, sitting down on a chair. "I was worried about you, this city's so unsafe at night," she said.

"Yeah, unsafe."

"Aren't you going to ask about Joyce?"

"Joyce?"

"My friend, Joyce."

"Oh, yes, Joyce. How is she?"

"Well, she's been better. Her mother's still very sick. The doctors aren't sure what's going to happen. It's a sad situation."

"Yeah . . . sounds sad."

"And Ken, you know, Joyce's husband, he called while I was there. Apparently he's going to be on the road for a week longer than he thought he'd be."

"Uh, that's too bad," said Bob.

"Yeah, that's what Joyce said, too. It's hard being alone all the time. Joyce was so happy that I came over. She said that I brightened her whole night."

"I'll bet."

"Huh?"

"I mean that she's lucky to have a friend like you."

"That's what she's always saying." Linda looked at her watch. "Well, I'm a little tired. I think I'll go to bed early tonight."

"Okay," said Bob.

Linda stood up and said, "I like Joyce a lot, but I must say that listening to all her problems can be a little tiring sometimes. Well, I'll say good night now."

"Night."

Linda smiled and then walked out of the living room. Bob stared at the wall for a couple of minutes, then, stood up, walked to the hall closet and opened the door. He reached into his jacket pocket and took out his gun. Then he walked into his workroom and closed the door.

He sat down at his desk, removed the bullets from the gun, then opened a drawer and placed the gun inside. He put the bullets back into their box and put the box near the gun. Then he closed the drawer and sat at his desk a while.

A little later, he got up and went into the bedroom. Linda was already asleep, a peaceful smile on her face. Bob got undressed and crawled into bed. It took him a long time to get to sleep and his dreams were not pleasant.

I have the strangest feeling we're being watched!

GLASS EYE

by Hal Charles

Kelly Locke gritted her teeth as "The Game's A-Foot" mug spilled coffee across her littered desk at WBAK-TV. It had been one of those days, and the young anchorwoman wondered if it were going to offer more evidence on the validity of Murphy's Law. Wasn't today supposed to be special? After all, it was Paul's birthday, and to celebrate she had planned to cook her boyfriend a very private and romantic dinner.

Getting home to prepare the meal—and herself—should have been easy. But that was before Chuck Mann, her co-anchor on Newsteam 4's *The 6:00 Evening News* had called in saying he was tied up with the flu—or, knowing Chuck, the floozy he couldn't bear to leave. Her two-year-old Tiburon with its ten-year warranty had conked out when she had pulled into the station's parking garage, and a freak electrical storm had disrupted the broadcast for twenty minutes. That's when a lightning bolt had struck her, making her overly aware that she had forgotten to buy the Metro's star centerfielder a birthday gift.

Finally she had caught a break or, at least, had thought so. Matt Locke, her father and the city's Chief of Detectives, had promised to swing by the station after his shift and give her a ride home. As she bounded out of the elevator in her London fog, she spotted his very obvious unmarked sedan. At least he was waiting and she could make it home just in time, even if she were without a present.

"Dad, you're a real lifesaver," Kelly said as she jumped into the seat and slammed the door ahead of a few raindrops. "And, don't worry, I am starting to fasten my seatbelt."

Pulling away from the curb, her slightly overweight father swallowed hard and said, "Honey, this'll only take a few minutes, but I just got a call on a 614 over on 8th and—"

"Don't tell me you're the nearest officer to a robbery." Kelly glanced out the window. "I can grab a cab—"

"Kelly, it's already raining cups on the way to buckets out there. I promise I'll get you home in time for your dinner. That Paul's a good one. If things work out, we'll have Metro box seats for life."

"Gee, for a second there, I thought you cared about my happiness." She laughed and sat back for the ride. Murphy had thrown her another curve.

Stepping under the Diamond-in-the-Rough canopy, Kelly's father opened the jewelry store door marked HENRI LAPORTE, PROP. for his daughter. A uniformed officer with a name-tag reading WHITE barred their entry and said loudly over the alarm, "Hold it, folks. This is police business."

Shaking his head, Matt Locke pulled his gold shield and I.D. from his blazer.

"Oh," White said, his face matching his name, "I didn't recognize you, Cap'n Locke."

"Dispatch was hazy," the Chief of Detectives said as White stepped out of their path. "What's going down?"

"I think it *has* gone down," said the uniform, his voice a bit shaky. "At first we thought it was a routine B&E, that someone had broken into our discount glasshouse here."

"Why?" said Kelly.

"My partner and me—he's the one over there with the clerk— just happened to be turning onto this block when the alarm went off. We couldn't have been more than a hundred feet away when we hit the siren."

"And then?" said Kelly.

"S.O.P. I covered the front. Rick, the side. We go by here enough to know there are only two ways out."

"How long exactly was your response time?" asked Kelly.

The officer looked at the anchorwoman as if a girl had just invaded his gang's secret clubhouse. "Listen, lady, you're not talking to a rookie." White clenched his nightstick. "We covered the exits in less than thirty seconds."

"What did you find?" she pressed.

"Nothing," snorted the uniform.

It was obvious to Kelly that White was uncomfortable answering questions from a woman, especially one who hadn't flashed gold.

"Nothing?" repeated her father.

Officer White gestured to the left of the jewelry store. "The side door opens into that alley, and the only way out of it is in the front. Nobody came out of the alley or the front door from the moment the alarm went off. I'll stake my badge on that."

"Any windows?" continued Kelly.

"Just the display in front, and as even you can see, it can't be opened." Officer White turned to Kelly's father. "Cap'n Locke, no disrespect, but who is this girl and why are you letting her grill me like some rookie fresh out of the academy?"

"This woman," said Matt Locke sternly, "is my daughter, and if Sherlock Holmes himself were here, he couldn't do any better figuring out what happened. But if you're going to get your shorts in a bind, I'll ask the questions. Now, is there a second story?"

"No, sir," snapped the chastised policeman.

"You searched the place?"

"We checked around a bit."

"And found nothing?"

"Just the clerk, who claims he was in the back room when the alarm went off. Said it must be faulty. You know, I got this smoke detector at home that goes off every time the little lady uses the stove to bake."

Kelly cringed as her father said, "Let's take a look around."

As they wound their way through the well-lighted maze of display cabinets, Kelly felt like Audrey Hepburn. Audrey had had Breakfast at Tiffany's, but it looked like Kelly was going to have to settle for a fast-food supper with her boyfriend.

They found the other uniform, Officer Rick Givan, standing by the bottled water cooler with a clerk whose sense of clothes coordination disqualified him for *GQ*. A striped tie hung over a plaid flannel shirt. Now inside, Kelly noticed the alarm's decibels seemed to have risen. "Can you turn off the alarm, Mr. LaPorte?"

"Eh, what," the clerk answered, straightening his tie, "but I'm not LaPorte, just an employee, and I'm new here."

From behind Kelly, White groused, "I told you he was a clerk."

Kelly ignored his attitude, but sensed her father getting a little short of patience.

"Officer White," addressed Captain Locke, "unless you'd like to pull an assignment checking dumpsters for discarded contraband, you'd better lighten up. Now why don't you and this employee go turn off the alarm."

"Sure thing, Cap'n. The darn thing's gone off before, and I know how to disengage it."

Kelly watched as the contrite officer and the clerk disappeared into the back room. She and Officer Givan crossed to the side door. "Your partner said you covered this exit," she said.

"Yes ma'am," answered the young officer in a voice made too loud by the abrupt end of the alarm.

Slipping on a glove from her purse so as not to disturb potential evidence, Kelly opened the door, where the storm had given way to occasional drops. Givan used his Maglite to paint the entire alley-way. Concertina wire surrounded the store's roof. The other alley walls were so high and without holds that even Spiderman would have gotten vertigo trying to climb them. "Wonder how they fix a leak in the roof," she mused aloud.

Givan said, "Workers can get up there through a skylight in the back room."

Kelly was impressed with the patrolman.

"We checked that too," said White. He was standing in the doorway carrying a flashlight and new respect. "It's bolted shut and covered with so many cobwebs nobody's been through it this decade."

Givan and Kelly re-entered the jewelry store. "Was this door locked when you got here?" she inquired.

"Tighter than a timpani," answered Givan.

"Just like the front, Miss Locke," chimed in the suddenly eager-to-please White.

The clerk, who was returning from the back room, bit off a piece of a Hershey bar and said, "Can we wrap this up? It's past 8:00, I don't get paid overtime, and I'm starved."

White shifted his bulky body to one side and patted his stomach like it had been a long time since his last meal. "What'd I tell you, Cap'n Locke? A clear case of false alarm. You ready to wrap up this present?"

Kelly turned to the clerk, who was wiping chocolate from the corner of his mouth with a handkerchief. "Mr. . . ."

"Hicks, Jack Hicks. My friends call me Bingo."

"Mr. Hicks, is there anything missing here?"

"Like I told the officers, I was in the back room and the front door was locked. I had to let these officers in, but I can check for you."

"Make it quick," said White. "My shift's over and the little lady likes to get out of the kitchen."

Not me, thought Kelly. She just wanted to get home to the kitchen. Paul would be arriving in less than an hour. She followed the clerk up and down the aisles till they came to a display case near the side door. Inside the case, the starkness of black velvet caught her eye. "What about this one?" Using her glove again, she pressed upward against the top of the case. It opened.

"Mr. LaPorte took the stones in there with him," said the clerk. "He has a buyer."

"Well, Cap'n," said White, turning abruptly toward the front door.

"File your report before you check out," said Matt Locke.

Suddenly Kelly got an idea. She grabbed one of the store's notepads with Diamond-in-the-Rough across the top of it. "I'm looking for a gift for my boyfriend," she said abruptly to Hicks. "Could you write down the price of your cheapest loose diamond so I can show him at least I was thinking of him?"

White shook his head. The clerk scribbled something and walked away. Kelly scrutinized what he had written: 1/4K—$450.

She jerked around. The clerk was passing in front of the water cooler, and the uniforms were starting out the front door. "Dad, grab Hicks."

Fifteen minutes later Matt Locke's face looked the way he had come up, empty. Kelly could see the lead story on *The Eleven O'Clock News.* "Chief of Detectives Facing False Arrest Suit!" Hicks hadn't had the diamonds on him.

Paul forked a piece of microwaved turkey breast. "I thought I had an exciting day hauling down that potential game-winning home run back onto the field, but it pales in comparison with—what did your dad call it?—collar." He separated the green beans from the meat. "Why did you suspect the clerk?"

Kelly pulled the price quotation out of her purse and let it float down into the good hands of the Metro's centerfielder. "Little things at first." As he studied the paper, she said, "What really happened earlier this evening was that Officers White and Givan interrupted a burglary in progress. To bypass the alarms, the thief had come into the busy store earlier in the day and hidden himself in the backroom. After the owner locked up, he came out. What he didn't know was that the display cases themselves are wired. When he opened one to grab some loose diamonds, the alarm was triggered."

"And before he could find the alarm to shut it off, the cops showed."

"Right. Our thief was a quick thinker when he heard the alarm. He slipped on a tie that the owner had left there—I noticed it clashed with his shirt—and pretended to be a clerk closing up. And then there was the alarm. If our supposed clerk knew it was false, why didn't he immediately shut it off when the officers arrived? Answer. He didn't know where the pad was and he didn't know the code."

"But you said he didn't have the diamonds on him and that the officers who searched the premises found nothing. Kel," added Paul with a smile, "if I came up that empty at the plate, I'd be a bench-warmer."

"That had me baffled for a while. There can't be a burglary unless something is stolen. A quick call to the store's owner, who hadn't gone to the coast, and LaPorte confirmed he had left on display some $200,000 in fine-cut white diamonds. As was his habit—something Hicks probably knew from observing him—he always closed up shop around seven, took a two-hour dinner at a downtown restaurant, and came back to put away some of the day's display in the store's safe. He liked to leave the stones on display for the passing dinner crowd." Hungry as she was, she gulped down more turkey, glad it wasn't crow. "Finally, LaPorte confirmed he had no clerk working for him that night or any other."

"Well done, Sherlock," said Paul across the candle-lit table, "but where were the diamonds?" He thumped the turkey breast with his fork. "There was no Christmas goose around to hide them in like in . . . what was that Doyle story you had me read last winter?"

"'The Adventure of the Blue Carbuncle.' These diamonds were hidden in plain sight, but nobody saw them. Maybe I caught on because the thief was near the water cooler both when I arrived and left. Officer White got a little wet when I had him lift the bottle from the stand and turn it over." Kelly smiled. "But when he did, the stones drifted through the water."

The baseball star looked like he had taken a called third strike. "The thief had stuck them in the water cooler?"

"It was easy. He just tipped the unit upside down, opened the spigot, dropped the stones in, and set the water cooler back in place. The whole operation took only a few seconds. He planned to con the officers into believing his faulty alarm story, show them to the door, then leave with the stones."

"But what if the cops spotted the diamonds?"

"Hicks panicked, but his spur-of-the-moment plan would have worked since flawless diamonds are invisible in water. I took a chance they were in the cooler even though I couldn't actually see them."

"Good guess, Kel, but how did this note make you suspect that the thief wasn't a clerk in the first place and cause you to place that cell phone call to LaPorte?"

"He turned out to be a minor-league second-story man, not some Cary Grant international cat burglar. He knew the basic value of the stones because he had to fence them, but look at that note again."

"1/4K—$450. So?"

"K is used to measure the worth of gold, something he also probably fences. K is short for karat. Diamonds, on the other hand, are measured with a C for carat. Even a first-day clerk in a jewelry store knows that."

"Well done, Kel."

She fidgeted with her fork. "Paul, I'm sorry I didn't have time to get you anything for a birthday gift."

Paul fixed his eyes on the blushing news anchor. "Gee, I thought nuked turkey breast was my gift. Seriously, just sharing tonight with you is enough gift for me. Besides, I learned something to-night."

She brushed her auburn hair out of her eyes. "What's that?"

"People who live in glass houses shouldn't stow stones."

Kelly never regretted throwing a bean toward the centerfielder's open mouth.

I want to report a stolen bathtub.

ANOTHER NIGHT TO REMEMBER

by William E. Chambers

My car was parked half a block away from the pub I own in Greenpoint Brooklyn, a 'Mixed-Use' Neighborhood of old apartment buildings, private homes, small shops and some heavy industry. All the surrounding businesses, except mine, closed early because it was Christmas Eve, and the shadowy street *seemed* deserted. But just as I stuck my key in the Oldsmobile's door, a voice from behind said, "Don't move. I'm holding a gun."

"I'm not moving," I assured the voice in as nonchalant a tone as I could muster. "What do you want?"

"Your money."

"I've got about three hundred bucks—" I felt something hard touch the back of my leather jacket, "in my pocket."

The voice patted me down from behind, found I was clean, and said, "Unlock the car. Front and back doors."

I opened the front door, reached over the seat and pulled up the button that locked the rear door of my aging Delta '88. The voice said, "Get in."

My unwanted companion climbed into the back seat while I slid behind the wheel. When both doors were locked, he explained, "We're gonna drive to a place with no phones. Then you're gonna get out and walk while I ride away in this heap with your money."

The face in the rear view mirror was pale, early thirties, and somewhat familiar-looking. The fact that he didn't mind my seeing his features bothered me. He asked if I knew the West Street piers and when I told him I did, he named a certain one and ordered me to take him to it. My mind spun like tires on ice as I began driving. I prayed a police car would pass by so I could plow this hunk of steel into it. None did. I thought of doing the same thing to any car at all but felt it was too risky. While he might hesitate to shoot me if cops were involved, I wasn't sure civilians would be a deterrent.

He might even kill them.

West Street was poorly lit and empty of cars and people. When I turned down the block leading to the pier, he said, "So far, so good, Callahan. You can stop at the edge of the dock."

The beauty of Manhattan's luminous skyline on the other side of the East River did nothing for my frayed nerves. Wood planking creaked beneath my tires and abandoned warehouses formed dark shapes along the Brooklyn shoreline to my right and left. Wind buffeted my car. Aside from the two of us, the area was devoid of life. A condition I expected myself to be in if I didn't do something quick. So I stomped the gas pedal and dived down, wedging my body between the seat and the dashboard.

A roar rocked the car. I saw sparks above my head and an acrid smell filled the air. The windshield webbed while my front tires bounced over the lip of the pier. Another shot rang out and the windshield disintegrated as the car flipped over. The man behind me hit the roof with his head and shoulders, dropping his weapon as the Olds slapped water. Then he thrashed about, screaming wildly in fear of the river that rushed in through the shot-out windshield below me. Knowing there was no bucking this icy torrent, I held my breath and waited. I was pounded repeatedly by a world that was cold and black and wet. When the force suddenly stopped, I heard the plunk of an escaping bubble and felt the car float downward.

Clawing blindly, I found the steering wheel and pulled myself toward the missing windshield. I tasted salt water and crude oil as I shoved my torso through the gap and kicked my feet against the fender of the descending car to begin my desperate upward swim. The blazing red and green Christmas lighting that adorned the Empire State Building's peak welcomed me to the surface from all the way across the river. I sucked in freezing air and paddled to a slimy piling. Somehow I managed to shinny up that greasy pole and scramble onto the dock.

I knew civilization wasn't far off but it seemed beyond my reach as I trudged forward on quivering legs. It was only three blocks, but the walk seemed to take forever because I had to stop several times to ease my burning lungs. Finally, I saw the kielbasa laden window of a Polish delicatessen whose dim lights indicated the store was about to close. I staggered through the front door and said, "I need your phone . . ."

The slender blonde-haired lady who was emptying the cash register muttered something I didn't understand then switched to English addressing me with the Polish word for mister that sounded like, "Pon! What has happened to you?"

"Please . . ." My teeth were clicking. "Accident . . . almost drowned. Need a phone . . ."

She led me through long red curtains to a back room where an elderly gentleman with a white mustache eyeballed me curiously. The woman punctuated staccato sentences in Polish with agitated gestures. When she dropped her hands and inhaled deeply, he motioned me to a phone on the wall. I dialed a police captain named Crowley. Luckily, he was still in his office. I asked him to come and get me and told him I'd explain why later.

The Polish couple demanded I dry off and change clothes, and insisted I drink something hot. I thanked them for their kindness and promised I'd bring the clothes back freshly laundered. Then, while my hosts resumed closing, I sat at the kitchen table in their rear-store apartment, sipping a cup of tea and mulling over the events that led to this situation.

There are some ex's in my life. I'm an ex-husband to a woman named Amanda and I'm an ex-Lieutenant, having retired from New York's Finest after being shot, an experience that left me with an aversion to guns. What I am now is the owner and proprietor of *Callahan's Pub,* an Irish-styled establishment in the largest Polish enclave on America's East Coast. Now, like all good publicans, I follow the *Tavern-keeper's Holiday Custom* of spreading Yuletide cheer in the bars and restaurants of my colleagues in the food and beverage business. I accomplish this by having a drink or two with each of the owners in their establishments and they reciprocate by visiting me in mine. I kicked off this season of good tiding by making my first stop at an out-of-the-way place called *Connors' Corner* near the East River in Long Island City.

Barry Connors usually made his daily bread through the lunch and early evening trade springing from the factories and warehouses surrounding his saloon. So I was surprised when arriving there rather late one evening to see yuppies, hard rockers, punk rockers, and some people who looked like they were off their rockers milling about the bar and occupying all the tables along the wall. Two family tragedies within a year, coupled with my efforts to keep a heavily mortgaged business afloat, kept me from socializing, so I didn't keep up with the changes here. A young lady bartender with long brown hair and what seemed to be two rockets stuffed into her sweater approached me, smiled and said, "Hi."

"I will be," I told her, "if I drink too much."

Her smile flashed brighter and was highlighted by a full, throaty laugh. Then she asked, "Now, what can I do to get you started drinking?"

"Scotch on the rocks is a good way to go."

"You've got it."

"Is Barry around?"

She shook her head and set up my drink. "Hasn't been in yet."

I thanked her, sipped some scotch and studied the crowd from a professional standpoint, what you might call an owner's point of view. It wasn't long before I spotted some strange goings-on. I noticed a tall, thin gentleman of olive complexion prancing in and out of the kitchen, which was located in a room to the side at the end of the bar. He brought out dishes of chips and pretzels, which the lady bartender distributed. He also made very frequent trips to the men's room, which was next to the lady's room across the floor from the kitchen.

During the course of an hour, I saw three new customers enter the bar. Within minutes of each arrival, Olive Skin would saunter into the gentleman's lavatory, stay briefly, then return to the kitchen. The recently arrived patron would soon make for the john himself. When he returned, Olive Skin would go back in.

I slowly nursed another two drinks and noticed the same thing happen when two young females walked in. While they sipped their drinks at the bar, Olive Skin returned to the men's room. When he came back, a young man sitting alone at a table went to the john then came back and sat down. Minutes later, the young ladies at the bar waved to the loner and acted as if they were surprised to see him. He seemed just as astonished at their presence and motioned them to join him at the table. Meanwhile, Olive Skin went back to the can. So I got up, walked over to the pay phone located in the alcove between the bar's double door entrance and dialed Barry

Connors' home number. When he didn't answer, I returned to the bar, paid for my drinks and left.

I phoned Barry several times over the next few days and caught him at home the night before Christmas Eve. When he answered my ring, I said, "Barry, I've got to talk to you about something very important. Are you free right now?"

"Sure, Marty. Come on over."

Barry lived in a converted loft above a furniture storage warehouse in an industrial section of Astoria, Queens. Pressing the intercom, I exchanged greetings with him before he buzzed me into the hall. Then I climbed a long flight of wooden steps and found him waiting in his open doorway. When we shook hands, I could see by his red-veined complexion that he was over-sampling his most toxic in-house products. He had a bar in his apartment that was almost as long as the commercial one he made his living from. Thumbing me toward it, he said, "Come in. Let me fix you a drink."

"Sure."

"What'll ya' have?"

"Beer's fine."

I straddled a stool and made room on the bar by shoving some racing forms aside. Barry ambled behind and opened a frosted brown bottle from the refrigeration unit below, then handed it to me. He poured himself a double sour mash and raised a toast to the season. I clinked my bottle to his tumbler and said, "Merry Christmas."

"And a Happy New Year to you, Martin, my boy. Glad you're out and about after all the family troubles."

"Life must go on," I sipped my beer and he downed his Jack Daniel's.

"Very true. God's will."

"I stopped by your place a couple of nights ago, Barry. Joint was jumping."

"Trade's picked up a lot since I hired Cynthia."

"Is that the lady with the long brown hair?"

Barry refilled his glass. "That's Cynthia."

"Who's the tall skinny guy with the olive complexion?"

"You must mean Faro. He's her boyfriend. Why?"

"I hate to be the bearer of bad tidings Barry, but he's dealing drugs."

The glass in Barry's hand never made it to his lips. "What?"

"Cocaine, probably."

"Cocaine!"

"You should pop in on your help when they don't expect it, pal. Hell, you taught that rule to me."

Barry lowered his glass, compressed his lips into a tight line and ran a set of pudgy fingers through his thinning white hair. "Marty, are you sure of this?"

"Before I bought the pub I was a detective and I haven't forgotten my training. You never lose your experience, you know."

"Guess you're right about that," Barry nodded and knocked back the drink.

"Faro's action's slick enough to fool the untrained eye, but when something's shady, *I* spot it."

After I explained Faro's routine, he said, "No wonder business has been so good lately."

"Barry, a little over a year ago drug dealers killed my nephew with their crap, although . . ." I swallowed hard and forced myself to tell the truth, "nobody forced him to indulge. Still, I hate these drug-dealing slime-bags. Look, I can help you with this. Remember Captain Crowley?"

Creases formed on Barry's forehead. "That detective friend of yours?"

"More like a close acquaintance. When I was on the job I helped him crack an insurance fraud case that spanned his precinct in Queens and mine in Manhattan South. So he feels he owes me. I could have him stake your place out and bust this operation."

"The scandal would ruin my business." Barry sighed and shook his head. "Who else knows about this, Marty?"

"Nobody."

"Not even your girlfriend?"

"No. Tammy's in Florida. Visiting her aunt. Comes home tomorrow night. I'm picking her up at LaGuardia. Nine p.m. flight."

"Look, don't tell her—or anyone. I'll take care of this myself."

"Are you sure—"

"I'm sure." Barry blinked thoughtfully. "Just leave it to me."

"Okay. But if you need help, call. You showed me the ropes when I opened my business and I don't forget favors."

"You don't have to tell me that, Marty." Barry reached out and shook my hand. "I know what a memory you have."

The sound of Captain Crowley's voice out front snapped me out of my reverie. When he walked into the kitchen, I greeted him wearing a sweatsuit, wool robe and fur-lined slippers. He looked me up and down, then said, "Where's the brandy and cigars?"

"Forgive me if I don't see the humor in that, Captain," I answered, biting back a chuckle in spite of my condition. "I'll explain everything while you drive me home."

I told Captain Crowley about Tammy's incoming flight, so he radioed for a patrol car to meet her at the airport, then drove away from the curb saying, "Okay, let's hear it."

Tammy walked into my apartment mortified at having been picked up by two uniformed police officers at LaGuardia. She thought it was my idea of a stupid joke. But when I told her about my chariot drop into the brine, her wide brown eyes stared at me without blinking. Captain Crowley settled his long lean frame onto my sofa and stared at me as well. His gaze seemed to say, "Are you going to tell her the rest of it?"

I nodded to him and I told her my thoughts.

I buzzed Barry Connors and announced my unexpected visit over his intercom. I explained I had placed an order for bar goods with my Queen's supplier and thought I'd stop by since I was in the neighborhood, anyway. When I walked through his door, he pumped my right hand and said, "I'm glad you're all right, Marty."

The tabloids picked up the story of my ordeal from Captain Crowley. I spoke to a couple of reporters as well. Now the word on the street was that nobody carjacks Marty Callahan and gets away with it. I reinforced that idea by saying to Barry, "That lowlife, whoever he is, won't rob any more."

Barry waved me toward the bar. "Some way to die."

"Better him than me."

"You're a hard man, Callahan," Barry laughed. "I read that he had no identification on him. That right?"

"Yeah."

"Beer?"

"I think a scotch will do me tonight."

"Scotch for you. Jack Daniel's for me." Barry poured the drinks, handed me a tumbler and touched his to mine. "Wish you told me you were stopping by tonight."

I emptied the glass, then asked, "Why?"

"Would've thrown a party to celebrate the fact that you're alive," he grinned. "Guess we'll have to party alone."

"Wish my nephew Rodney could be here to party with us."

"Ah, yes. Your nephew was a good kid. Smart kid. I mean, became a Wall Street Broker, no less." Barry shook his head sadly. "God rest him."

"*And* one of your best customers when he wasn't mastering the financial world, if I remember right."

"True. We talked a lot. He thought the world of you, Marty. He said he'd always owe you for helping put him through school."

"My brother-in-law David died of a massive heart attack when Rod was a baby. Dave owned a flower shop that was just getting off the ground on borrowed money. Left nothing but bills behind. So, I had to help. Rod and my sister Loretta were the only relatives I had left. When she lost Rod, Loretta fell into a depression and never really recovered."

"Seems I remember you taking her to therapy."

"Yeah. It seemed to work—for a while. Then one night, she swallowed a bottle of pills . . ."

"Sadly, I remember. Didn't know her well. But your nephew always ran errands for me until he went off to college." Barry laughed. "I kept him employed as a kid just like you asked me to."

"That's right. I introduced him to you and he liked you and trusted you and it was probably your coke that blew out the blood vessels in his head."

My host continued pouring a new round but his bushy white eyebrows knitted together. "What are you saying?"

"*You're* running drugs," I thrust my forefinger so close to his face I damn near poked his eye. "And you put a hit on me."

"That car dive—" Barry rolled his eyes, "must have rattled your brain."

"Why'd you go into the drug business? Are you addicted?"

"Addicted!" Barry spat the answer out. "Sure!"

"Gambling debts, then? Are you in over your head?" I gestured toward the racing forms. "Sure looks like it."

"Why . . . after all I've done for you!" Barry's rising voice was filled with indignation. "Get the hell out of here! Go or I'll call the cops!"

"No need. You'll be seeing plenty of cops in the future."

"And what is that supposed to mean?"

"I'm going to ask my NYPD colleague Captain Crowley to send you some business. Nothing official. Just some off duty officers who like to drink and hang around and watch things."

"You mean you haven't asked him all ready?"

"No. Because I wasn't sure about your complicity before."

"But you're sure now?"

"Dead certain."

"And why's that?"

"That gunman who took me for a ride looked familiar. And the reason he looked familiar has been haunting me until just now when you poured my drink. It just dawned on me that he was one of the yuppies I had seen in your bar."

"Nonsense!"

"Captain Crowley won't think it's nonsense. His watchdogs will either put you in jail or—"

Barry leaned forward, his right hand disappearing under the bar. "Or what?"

"Or you'll clean up your act and I'll have the satisfaction of knowing I ruined your dirty little business."

"All right. If you must know, it was *my* cocaine that did your nephew in, Marty." Barry's hand came up clutching a snub nosed .38. "Seems his blood pressure couldn't handle it. But like you said yourself, nobody forced him to take it. He even brought me Wall Street trade."

"If I had known, Barry, I would have straightened him out and my sister would be alive today."

"No way would you've straightened him out. Success made your nephew cocky. But I'm going to straighten you out."

"By shooting me with that revolver?"

"Why not? Must protect my enterprise, Marty. This area's deserted at night. My friends will make you disappear later. And who'll be the wiser?"

"The police. I'm wired."

"Wired?" The color drained between the whiskey lines in his face. "I don't believe it."

"Look!" I yanked up my shirt and showed him the bug taped to my side. "The truth about your half-assed hit-man *really* dawned on me right after I went for that nerve-wracking ride. I thought about how that gunman frisked me for a weapon, and called me by name. Then I remembered seeing him in your bar. After that, I knew you set me up for a carjacking gone awry. Cops would be chasing teenage stickup artists and never connect to the drug trade. Very neat."

We were both startled by the crash of the vestibule door downstairs. When the intercom buzzed as well, Barry closed his eyes and sighed. The sight of my forty-eight-year-old sister laid out in her casket just months ago flashed through my mind. Something twisted in my stomach as I said, "You're ship is sinking, pal. What was the first Titanic movie? *A Night To Remember?* Well, this is another night to remember."

That remark wrenched Barry. His eyes snapped open and a shiver ran through him. I seized his gun-hand and, as I bent it away from me, one of my fingers slipped through the trigger guard. The roar plugged my eardrums and the flash stung my eyes. Barry fell from my grasp. I squinted several times, swallowed hard and shook my head. Once I refocused, I saw him lying, blood-spattered, behind the bar. Footsteps pounded up the stairs and two uniformed cops, guns drawn, burst in. Captain Crowley was right behind them. He looked about, then said, "What happened?"

"Barry panicked. Started waving the gun. So I tried to grab it. Next thing I knew, he was dead on the floor."

Crowley shot me an odd look, then shrugged. "One less case for our overburdened legal system."

The police raided Connors' Corner that very night and found quite a stash of narcotics hidden around the premises. Faro was wedging packets of cocaine between the toilet tank and the wall in the men's room when Crowley nailed him. Obviously the customers would close the stall door, remove the product and replace it with cash. But Cynthia had nothing on her person and she denied everything, saying the goods must belong to Barry. The Captain later persuaded Cynthia that she could do time, anyway, then convinced the District Attorney to grant her immunity if she flipped. So she turned "State's Evidence" against the love of her life. Faro's going to do some heavy time, according to Captain Crowley's prediction. It also came out in court that Barry, my friend of many years, succumbed to his gambling addiction and owed his existence to bookies and loan sharks, one of whom had taken me for a ride. Barry chose to redress his problems by selling cocaine. Tammy feels justice was satisfied somewhat but that it's grossly unfair for Cynthia to walk away free. I agreed, saying, "Sometimes people just get away with murder in this city."

✗

Beware Macduff. And cut down on carbs.

THE PERFECT (PART-TIME) FOIL

by Jean Paiva

Sydell Davis drained the last of her cold Collins, its redolent juniper flavor particularly soothing to her parched throat. Grateful for the relief from dryness as much as the easing of bunched muscles and taunt nerves, she pushed the glass away. Even more important to Sydell, she was grateful that this was the only drink she now wanted—one, each day, after work.

Glancing at the kitchen clock, Sydell hurried to gather her belongings in the large tote bag. Keys, wallet, cosmetic case, comb, tissues, a miscellaneous pile (not yet inventoried but surely needed), an apple—no, make that two, both the kids would want one—and, finally, dark glasses—the sun seemed oddly bright of late.

And, she reminded herself, don't forget to hang the uniform out to air. The sulfur stench was at its worst when she stood downwind from the plant and this morning, positioned directly down-wind, the fumes had belched continuously. Sydell had been warned that end of the month quotas always increased production. Today's frantic activity, and lingering malodors, bore pungent witness to that fact.

Time to head to school and retrieve the twins.

The last drag on her unfiltered cigarette was sweeter than the first. Nicotine-saturated smoke smoothly entered Sydell's lungs and, holding the poisonously laced vapor for a full minute, she cleared the final traces of other, more fetid, odors from her respiratory system. Smiling, knowing it was well worth the trade, Sydell headed to her car.

Finding the twins waiting, already squabbling, was an added pleasure. The drive over had been luxurious. A turnpike accident, rich in greasy smoke, held up traffic for fifteen minutes. Fifteen minutes of stop and go traffic in the unusually hot, late-September sun. Fifteen minutes of breathing noxious carbon monoxide fumes inside a car that was threatening to overheat any second. Fifteen tranquil minutes of relative peace and quiet.

"I want that apple, it's bigger."

"No, I want that apple, it's got a leaf attached."

"I'm first, I was born first. I'm older."

"So what? I'm bigger and I want that apple."

"Charleene, Robert," Sydell gently intercepted the apple clutched by four small hands, "I can cut this apple in half or we can play a game and the winner gets all."

"In half," Charleene voted.

"No, a game!"

"You always win."

"You always get your way."

"No I don't, you do."

"A game," demanded Robert, "is fair."

"What kind of game," asked Charleene, already resigned to the smaller apple.

Sydell smiled at the twins, her heart filled near to bursting with love for them—scraped, dirty, torn tee-shirt, lost shoelaces and all. "How about a riddle?"

The twins shot a look at each other, grinning under their professed petulance.

"Sure," they simultaneously offered, "we're both good at riddles."

"Okay," Sydell said, glancing in the rear view mirror at her treasures. "Here goes: What's black and white and red all over?"

"Me first," Charleene volunteered. "That's easy. A newspaper."

"Well," Sydell signed, "I guess that's one answer. But not the one I had in mind. How about you, Bobbie, got an answer for your old Mom?"

"Yeah, I sure do," he answered with a sneer.

"Well, what is it? You're supposed to answer the riddle, I'm not supposed to figure out your answer."

"A racially mixed couple caught copulating by the Klan and slaughtered on the spot."

"Very *good*, Bobbie. Here, you get the apple," Sydell said as she tossed the prized fruit to her beaming son. Taking the smaller apple out for her daughter, she handed it over to the deflated girl and soothingly added, "Charley, this one is almost as big. Someday you'll be as precocious as your brother. You just have to try a bit harder, that's all dear."

Sydell drove on, mindless to the arguments erupting from the back seat. It was so encouraging to hear such vitality and purpose. Life was so different before she started working part-time. These wonderful sibling interactions once bothered her. Not so now. The darlings could do anything they liked, short of permanently disfiguring each other, and it was a true pleasure to behold. Fortunately, they were primarily into psychologically torturing each other and both were extremely inventive. Retelling the twin's antics made her very popular at break time.

"Are we going to pick up Daddy?" Robert asked, his mouth full of partially chewed apple.

"Don't talk with your mouth full, dear. It isn't polite," Sydell cautioned. "We're going home to make a wonderful dinner for your Daddy. Then we'll pick him up."

"What's for dinner?" Charleene asked.

"Daddy wasn't feeling well this morning, he had a bit of a tummy ache, so I thought I'd make something light. Let's have chili."

"I get to chop the peppers," Charleene volunteered while Robert still had his mouth full.

"Of course, dear. And, Bobbie, you can grate horse-radish for the salad," assigned Sydell, knowing both her precious offsprings would tackle their respective chores with care and diligence. "And I brought home something special from my job. The double-rich, double chocolate layer cake with fudge icing that you both love."

The squeals from the twins may have reached a decibel level painful to most but to Sydell it was music. Even her husband's particular choice of operatic arias, which used to sound like mindless caterwauling, were now melodious masterpieces.

Thinking back to a few short weeks ago, Sydell remembered how almost unbearable life had become. Her nerves had been frayed to the quick with the seemingly endless household chores and petty disruptions caused and embellished on by two active children and a husband who worked long, hard hours to keep them living stylishly in the prestigious community they called home.

A hobby, her mother had lovingly suggested, would provide both distraction and constructive occupation; a job, her husband had practically pointed out, would provide both diversion and additional income. A job, her mother had almost choked on the word, would imply to their neighbors a failure and inability to properly maintain one's lifestyle. A hobby, groaned her husband, would be another expense. Surprisingly, they had both resigned themselves to whatever Sydell chose to do, with the stipulation that she find *something* before she either had a breakdown or alcoholic lapse.

And find something to do she had definitely done.

It was chance that posted the notice on the supermarket bulletin board at eye level, her eye level being 5'7" in Nike running shoes. It was opportunity that caused the brown paper bag to burst open from a leaky milk carton leaving her standing, exasperated, staring blankly ahead rather than dealing with the already purchased mess at her feet. It was fate that brought together these disparate incidents and stranded Sydell with the notice pinned six inches from her nose.

Part Time Jobs
4 Hours a Day—Your Choice AM or PM
Good Pay. Easy Commute.
Crossing Guards—Redheads Preferred
Guaranteed to Make Your Day!

It was the Guarantee that caused Sydell, now empty-handed with squashed tomatoes underfoot, to tear off the paper tag bearing a local phone number. "If I weren't already auburn I'd run back for some Lady Clairol," she muttered to the dour assistant manager now standing next to her, his annoyance at the mess she'd made clearly written on his pinched face. Turning on her rubber heel and further mashing a pint of spilled blue berries, Sydell intentionally flicked her foot back—spraying berry juice on the market guardian's clean white uniform—and trotted out. Of course red hair would be preferred for a crossing guard, she had assumed with a newly defined singular purpose. It would be much easier to spot at a crossing.

At home she mixed herself a gin gimlet, the consumption of which once was required after shopping of any kind, and called the neatly typed phone number that, for some inexplicable reason, seemed to fade even as she punched in the numbers. A recording instructed her to leave her name, address, phone number and the hours she would like to work, and promised to get back to her very shortly. Before she had the gimlet glass washed, the doorbell rang.

A job was so much more fulfilling than a hobby, Sydell reflected. Besides, the hobbies she had tried were disasters—from lumps of clay that resembled dog feces to developing a unique knack for growing weeds—and the ones she would like to try weren't feasible. There were no mountains nearby to climb, even if she knew how, and directing snuff movies probably required some sort of film background. Best of all, the job paid well. Now she earned enough to make life a little easier and also found she was ten times more efficient, twenty times more relaxed, a hundred times more responsive and a thousand times more appreciative of her own home, family and life.

Fortunately the commute was so easy, Sydell thought as she pulled into her driveway. This '74 Pinto wagon, running on three cylinders, wasn't good for the long haul. Another month and the down payment on the brand-new, bright-red Thunderbird would be nested away; it was time to forgo station wagons for the sporting life, time to enjoy everything that life had to offer.

Uninterrupted bickering from the twins played in the background like a Brahms lullaby; the backfiring ancient power lawnmower across the street added percussion to the soothing rhythms sifting through her neighborhood. The Gordon's next door, now retired and at each other's throats ever since, were loudly proving that even after the golden fiftieth wedding anniversary couples could still find things to communicate about, albeit at the top of their lungs. What a comforting thought, Sydell realized; there was something more to look forward to. Humming softly as she unlocked the back door, Sydell herded the children into her warm and cozy kitchen.

"How about a piece of that devil's food cake with milk now, before dinner?" she offered.

The happy screeches from her beautiful babies reassured Sydell that again, as usual of late, she'd made a wise decision.

"Then we'll start dinner and pick up Daddy," she added, pouring two large glasses of heavily chocolated milk.

Some career women complained about their bosses, despite whatever benefits they claimed to gain from working. Angelia, even thinking her friend's name caused a grating at the base of Sydell's skull, professed to love her job at the art gallery. She said it afforded her many moments of reflection on the beauties of life, but hated her boss—whom she called a fiend. Angelia couldn't even begin to know the meaning of having a perfect foil, even part-time, to enforce the true bounties life had to offer. And, one thing Sydell was absolutely sure of, her friend did not have a fiend for a boss.

Sydell shook her head in wonderment as she busied herself in the kitchen, effortlessly lining up the ingredients for dinner. She was so lucky; her crossing guard job took so little time, four hours and five minutes including the commute—though it was a bit tougher getting home than getting there. It still was terrific the way they picked her up and brought her back. There was still a miraculous (the sharp stab at the base of her neck sent a shiver down Sydell's spine; she *would* get the hang of the terminology very soon) amount of time to whip through her chores.

The preparatory work complete, Sydell checked the clock and realized she was running a few minutes late. The twins' verve and vigor never ceased to amaze her; even with the simple chores assigned them they had managed to invent a spirited game involving the loser having chili peppers or horseradish (depending on who was preparing which and who lost) stuffed into their nostrils. Gathering up the children, she made ready to head for the railroad station to pick up Barry.

Ah, Barry, he of the tall trim torso still lusted after even now, fourteen years later. Desired even more now that her daily tensions and aggressions had an outlet. Last night, despite the onset of Barry's upset stomach—could it have been caused by the curry he said was fiery? Doubtful, as it was mild to her taste—was as good as their first time. During her indoctrination session for the crossing guard position they had alluded to improved sexual relations, relating it to the phenomena of a need to renew life, and cautioned her to stock up on birth control methods. Sydell was glad she had paid attention and that her medicine cabinet now stayed constantly full.

"How was your day, dear?" Barry solicitously inquired as he slid into the front passenger seat. Even Barry's attitude toward her had greatly appreciated. Once, just a few short weeks ago, he had rushed home and downed two or three properly chilled martinis before he said anything halfway intelligent to her. Now, ever since she had begun to share the wonders of her crossing guard job—telling cute anecdotes, talking about co-workers and supervisors, and *especially* relating her deep inner thoughts and feelings about how much she enjoyed her work—he treated her with, well, respect.

While he seemed to blanch at the description of the dinner that awaited him, Barry's bright smile belied any doubts she had about his sincerity in that the chili was just what he was looking forward to.

And he did justice to eating every last morsel, though he blamed the greenish cast of his skin to the new fluorescent lighting at work.

Children tucked in, husband reading a book—what was that title? His thumb covered all but "Daniel Webster"—Sydell began preparations for the morning. Getting the family out early used to be a chore but now, knowing that she'd be picked up for work as soon as everyone was gone, breakfast was the best time of day. Coffee pot ready to be plugged in, table set with cereal bowls, her uniform—still airing outside!

Carefully removing the jacket and slacks from the clothes-line, Sydell brought her uniform into the kitchen. For some reason, the sight of it in the morning seemed to evoke unease in Barry, though not the children, but hanging it next to the refrigerator served as a pleasant reminder that she would soon be back in control again. The shiny metal buttons, with the traditional pitchfork logo etched on each, gleamed against the soft black leather of the jacket; the supple leather matching slacks zippered merrily up each leg and were most becoming. The *piece de resistance* was carefully folded in the jacket pocket; it was understandable that her high-tensile strength whip would make the children nervous, not that she'd ever use it on them.

It got enough use during her shift; performing duties, exorcising (damn that demonic twinge, thought Sydell) aggressions and executing (now, there was a good word) her supervisors' instructions. And with her brilliant auburn hair she perfectly matched the vibrant decor she worked in, even to the hooks suspended from the ceiling.

The only flaw in this otherwise perfect arrangement was so minor that she berated herself for even thinking about it. But, with less time now for household chores it was the one thing that threw her schedule off. When they picked her up for work, why in hell did they have to burn open her kitchen floor, even temporarily, for her to chute down? It always left ashes all over the place.

✗

MISS PODSNAP'S PEARLS

by Roberta Rogow

Most visitors to Deauville came to get away from their lives. Miss Podsnap came to find hers.

The little fishing village on the coast of Normandy had become a magnet, drawing the aristocratic world when the putative brother of the Emperor Napoleon II had decided to construct a race-course there. With the fall of the Emperor, the nobility went elsewhere for amusement, but bourgeois holiday-makers were able to visit the coast via the newly-built railways. Moreover, the English were able to cross the Channel in regular steamers, and swelled the numbers of visitors to such hotels as the Grand National, a sprawling pile with access to both the beach and the town.

To this resort came Miss Georgiana Podsnap. She marched into the Grand National Hotel with an odd air of defiance, followed by a grim-faced middle-aged maid. Miss Podsnap had once been a gawky adolescent, given to hiding her elbows and cringing in corners. She was now a gawky woman approaching forty, wearing an unfashionably full-skirted English walking-dress in the pale grey and mauve of half-mourning, topped with a black straw hat decorated with a gray ribbon.

M. Renard, the manager of the hotel, came forth to greet her. He made it his business to check the credentials of new arrivals. Miss Podsnap, according to his sources, had just inherited a tidy fortune from her late father, a gentleman well known in London Society. She had no immediate relations, there were no entails or other encumbrances upon her inheritance, and she appeared to be traveling with only her maid as companion. M. Renard knew of several gentlemen who would appreciate an introduction to Miss Podsnap. He bowed ingratiatingly, then recognized the young lady who had stepped forward to greet Miss Podsnap.

"Bonjour Mademoiselle Podsnap," M. Renard said, beaming at her. "We 'ave been expecting you."

"Bon Jour," Miss Podsnap said, trying to recall the words she had learned before taking her unprecedented trip abroad.

Before she could go on, she was interrupted by the object of M. Renard's consternation. "Miss Podsnap?" the young lady asked. "I was asked by Mr. Lightwood to meet you here. I am Miss Venn."

"Mr. Lightwood told me that he had arranged for an acceptable guide," Miss Podsnap said. "He did not mention that the guide would be female."

Miss Venn shrugged. "I speak both French and English, and I have lived in France most of my life. I suppose Mr. Lightwood thought that he would do both of us a good turn, since I am in need of employment, and you are in need of a translator."

"I see." Miss Podsnap looked the girl over. Miss Venn was shorter than she, and considerably plumper, with a distinctive arch to her nose in an otherwise round face. She was fashionably dressed in the most current style, with a narrow skirt under a severely-cut overdress, and only a flat bow at the base of the spine instead of the elaborate bustles that were now deemed dowdy. The dress itself may have been new, Miss Podsnap observed to herself, but the fabric showed signs of having been used before in a previous incarnation as a much fuller skirt.

"Will Madamoiselle Podsnap be taking her meals in the restaurant?" M. Renard inquired, leading the party to the front desk where they could be properly registered, and given their keys.

"Is it the custom for a lady to dine in public in France?" Miss Podsnap asked Miss Venn. "I know my Papa would have been most distressed if he thought I was acting improperly, but this is France, after all, and not London."

"It is quite respectable for a lady to dine in a restaurant in Deauville," Miss Venn replied. "Of course, in Paris, things are somewhat different. I can explain matters to you in more detail while your maid unpacks your bags."

"I only brought the one portmanteau with me," Miss Podsnap said diffidently. "Mr. Lightwood thought I should purchase clothes in Paris. I have not been out of mourning for so very long, first for my Grandmama, then poor Mama, and then Papa. Perhaps I should find something more, um . . . ."

"Festive?" Miss Venn suggested. The maid coughed meaningfully. "Oh, yes, Jane. There is really no reason to be distressed."

Miss Venn eyed the small leather case the maid clutched fiercely to her gaunt person. "Is that a jewel-case?"

"Mama always said that chits and jewels don't go together, so I never wore anything but the little locket that Papa gave me, and Grandmama Hawkins' small enamel brooch. However, I brought Mama's diamonds, and the pearl set. I can wear those with half-mourning, at least, until I get something more decorative."

"They should be placed in the hotel vault for safe-keeping," M. Renard stated.

"But then I would not have them to make my selection," Miss Podsnap demurred. "No. I shall keep them in my room, where I shall hide them."

Miss Venn glanced around the crowded lobby of the hotel. Miss Podsnap did not use the ringing tones of most English tourists abroad, who went on the assumption that anyone could understand English if one spoke it loudly enough, but her voice did carry, and there was a noisy family of Americans crowding in behind her. Perhaps this was what Mr. Lightwood meant when he wired her to "keep an eye on Miss Podsnap."

M. Renard beckoned the uniformed porter, who led Miss Podsnap's party up the grand staircase to a second floor room that overlooked the Channel. He stood expectantly, hand outstretched, until Miss Venn coughed meaningfully. Then Miss Podsnap produced a coin from her reticule, and the porter grimaced and vanished.

Miss Venn peeked out the window. "I see they gave you one of the rooms they use for English and American guests, the ones that look out on the sea. The French won't have a breath of air in their rooms, so stuffy, but the English insist on fresh air. You've got a lovely view, even though you're right over the veranda."

Miss Podsnap turned to the younger woman. "You mentioned that Mr. Lightwood communicated with you about my coming to France. How do you know Mr. Lightwood?"

"He is my Trustee, under the terms of my godfather Twemlow's Will," Miss Venn replied, with another Gallic shrug.

"Mr. Twemlow?" Miss Podsnap echoed. "How odd."

Miss Venn went on, "I never even knew I had a godfather until Mama wrote to him, after the Prussians left France. Papa had gone to Paris, and most of Mama's jewels had gone with him, and we were left in a very bad way. If it hadn't been for Mr. Twemlow's little legacy, and his paying for my schooling, I do believe we would have starved. I only wish I could have met him, but as I understood it, he was quite elderly, and in poor health."

Miss Podsnap recalled the little man in outmoded evening clothes who lived on a tiny annuity and dined at Society tables on the strength of his aristocratic connections, and said nothing. Mr. Twemlow had been instrumental in removing her from the influence of a pair of rogues, one of whom was the only friend she had ever had.

"Now then," Miss Venn said briskly, "what exactly do you wish to do, Miss Podsnap? Mr. Lightwood explained in his letter to me that you were just out of mourning, and wanted to see a bit of the world. Deauville is rather thin of company in May, what with the London and Paris Seasons in full swing, as the Americans have it, but there are the theatres, and the shops, and possibly the Casino, if you choose to take a flutter."

Miss Podsnap considered the itinerary. "I will dine in the restaurant this evening, Miss Venn. Tomorrow I will walk on the shore, and I do want to look in the shops. Are you staying here at this hotel, Miss Venn?"

"My Mama and I are in a *pension* in another part of the town," Miss Venn explained. "There is another English lady who stays there, and assists me with my mother, who is sometimes. . . difficult. If it would be more convenient, I suppose you could arrange for me to share the room with your maid, in the servants' quarters."

"You aren't a servant," Miss Podsnap decided. "You are my companion. I shall pay your expenses, of course, and we shall see how we get on."

Miss Venn nodded. "Of course, Miss Podsnap. And since Mr. Lightwood recommended that I should advise you, I must tell you that you should not leave your jewel-case lying about. There are thieves, even in the best hotels."

"I don't think any thieves would look at my jewels," Miss Podsnap said. "The diamonds are very small, but the pearls are quite nice, I've been told. Jane?"

The maid stepped forward, still clutching the leather-covered box. Miss Podsnap produced a small key from her reticule, and opened it to reveal the contents: a double strand of pearls, earrings and a brooch to match.

"I shall wear them tonight," Miss Podsnap announced. "Miss Venn, will you please make whatever arrangements you think suitable, for two ladies to dine this evening. Jane, I shall wear the mauve evening dress."

Miss Venn recognized a dismissal when she heard one, and left mistress and maid to deal with the problems of dressing for dinner. She herself would have to cross the town, and explain to Mama that she would not be able to dine with them. She only hoped that Sophronia would be able to cope with Mama alone.

Miss Venn joined Miss Podsnap at the restaurant, wearing the aforementioned mauve gown, decorated with the same silver lace that rested on her sandy hair. The pearls gleamed on her neck and ears, and the brooch held the lace in place to cover the décolletage of the gown. Miss Venn herself wore an evening dress of deep gold that contrasted well with her auburn hair. The two ladies were seated in an alcove, well away from the more fashionable center of the dining room, where Miss Podsnap hoped to be inconspicuous.

This was not to be. The stout woman at the table next to them was the very American who had crowded upon them at the hotel desk, and she peered at Miss Podsnap's pearls with the eye of an expert.

"I must say, I've never seen the like of them pearls!" she crowed. "And I've seen a pearl or two in my time, what with my Pa being in the oyster business.

"I'm Mrs. Magill," she added, by way of introduction. "And I heard your name at the desk, when we was checking into this place, Podsnap, ain't it?"

"Mother!" The young lady at the table turned pink with mortification. "You can't just talk with anybody!"

"Well, that's why we're here, ain't it? To meet people? And as for your Grandpa's profession, well, if it wasn't for his boats, Magill would never have looked twice at me, and you and your brother wouldn't be here. This is my daughter Judith, and that's my son, George."

Nods were exchanged. Miss Podsnap turned her attention back to her dinner. Mrs. Magill was still chattering.

"I tell you, ma'am, you should put them pearls in a real safe place. I've heard about them thieves in French hotels."

"Oh, I don't think I have to worry. My maid has a very good place to hide the box, right where I can find it."

The Magill clan went on eating, and Miss Podsnap and Miss Venn left the restaurant for a stroll on the terrace. From beyond the veranda came the sounds of the Casino: the whirr of a roulette wheel, the cries of the gamblers. Through the long French windows Miss Podsnap noticed young Mr. George Magill among the seekers of fortune. From the look on his face, he wasn't finding any.

"Would you care to try your luck, Miss Podsnap?" Miss Venn asked.

"Oh no, I don't think so. Mama used to play whist for shilling points, and Papa did not like it at all. He preferred to venture on the Exchange, and did rather well by it." Miss Podsnap frowned into the darkness. "Who is that woman?"

Miss Venn looked into the shadows at the side of the Casino. "Oh dear, I am very sorry, Miss Podsnap, but I must leave you now. That is my mother. She comes here sometimes, to look at the English visitors. She must have slipped away from our friend, who looks after here. She can sometimes be. . . difficult. I will take her back to our *pension* and I can join you here tomorrow."

"Sophia! Baby!" The woman in the shadows called out. "Those are my pearls! That woman is wearing my pearls!"

"No, Mama, they are her pearls," Miss Venn said, steering her mother away from the lights, and leaving Miss Podsnap to find her own way back to her room, where Jane was waiting for her.

"Have you spoken with any of the other servants?" Miss Podsnap asked, as her maid undid the hooks of her dress.

"Yes, Miss Georgiana, but most of 'em are Frenchies, so I didn't get much out of 'em. The Americans, Mrs. Magill and her daughter, they've got a darky woman with them, who speaks some kind of French. Young Mr. George, he don't have a man, and he does for himself mostly."

Miss Podsnap stared into the dressing-table mirror as Jane undid the pins that held her hair in place, and began to brush. "Jane, do you recall when you came to me?"

"Right after you was out, Miss Georgiana. Your Mama said you needed a steady ladies' maid."

"Do you recall some people named Veneering?"

Jane stopped brushing briefly. "Oh. Them. Only thing I can recall is that they ran off and didn't pay their servants. A right scandal that was!"

"My Mama and Papa dined with them," Miss Podsnap said. "They sometimes included me, when they needed to make up the numbers. They gave very grand parties." Miss Podsnap remembered her own introduction to Society, a dinner party at which she was largely forgotten until one woman had spoken to her and made her a part of the Veneering's social circle.

"You may go, Jane," Miss Podsnap said. "I shall not need you until tomorrow morning. Miss Venn will take me out tomorrow, and perhaps I will go to the theatre. Good night."

Miss Venn appeared early the next morning, apologizing profusely for her mother's untimely appearance. The two ladies spent a cheerful morning walking on the beach, followed by a brief luncheon at one of the many small cafes that lined the streets of the part of Deauville that catered to the tourists. Mrs. Magill and her daughter were very much in evidence, bustling from shop to shop, loudly praising or condemning the merchandise. The four ladies fell into step as they returned to the Grand National Hotel.

"Did you find anything nice, Miss Podsnap?" Mrs. Magill inquired.

"I don't think I am quite ready to order a French gown," Miss Podsnap said. "Miss Venn, I noticed that tea is served in the lounge. I shall change my dress, and then we shall have tea."

"As you say, Miss Podsnap."

Miss Podsnap ascended the grand staircase, only to return within minutes. "I wish to speak to the manager at once," she announced. "My pearls are missing."

"Missing? Are you sure?" Miss Venn asked.

"I mean exactly what I said. I went to the wardrobe, where Jane had placed the box with the pearl set, and the box was gone."

M. Renard emerged from his office, all excited bluster and French effusion. Such a thing had never happened in his establishment! It must have been the maids, although he would have sworn to all the saints in Heaven that they were good country girls, who would never steal from guests at the Grand National Hotel.

"Are you going to call the police?" Miss Podsnap asked.

M. Renard recoiled in horror. "The police? In my hotel? What an idea!" If Miss Podsnap would rest tranquilly and have a cup of good English tea, all would be settled. He would question the maids immediately.

Miss Podsnap would not be bought off with tea. "I will speak with the persons who make up the rooms myself," she stated. "May we use your office, sir? It would be less public."

With Miss Venn trailing behind her, Miss Podsnap was led to the manager's office. Shortly thereafter, two stout young women in the striped skirts and white linen blouses favoured by the servants of the Grand National Hotel appeared, one truculent, one nervous. In heavily-accented Norman French they denied seeing any leather-bound box anywhere in the room assigned to Miss Podsnap.

"I arrange the pillows, I arrange the sheets, I arrange the coverlet," declared the truculent girl, Marie-Claire.

Annette, the nervous girl, added, "I dust the armoire, I dust the dressing-table, I remove the water from the pitcher and replace it with fresh."

"Did you open the armoire?" Miss Podsnap asked.

"For why should I do so? I am not to look inside the armoire, but to dust and polish the outside, and so I do."

"Of course," Miss Podsnap said with a nod. "And when you had finished your tasks, what did you do then?"

"We went on to clean the rooms of the Americans, Madame Magill and her son and daughter," replied Marie-Claire, who was the more forthcoming of the two.

"Did you see anyone in the corridor who should not have been there? No strangers?" M. Renard put in, anxious to play a part in the investigation.

"No one who should not have been there, no," Marie-Claire said. "The servant of Madame Magill, she told us that she would arrange the rooms of Madame to her particular liking, and that we need not bother ourselves about them. She is a woman of colour, you understand, and very fierce, so we did not dare to go against her wishes."

Miss Podsnap thought for a moment, then asked, "Do you recall whether you left the window open or closed when you left my room?"

The two maids looked blankly at her. Then Annette said, "I believe I closed the window, Madamoiselle. The sea air, it is not good for the health in large amounts, and must be taken carefully."

"That is most interesting," said Miss Podsnap, "because I left the window closed this morning when I went out, but you now tell me that the window was open when you arrived. You then closed it, but the window was open when I came into the room this afternoon. A window does not open and close itself. Someone must have come in and out of that room, either before or after the maids finished their work."

"I am not a thief!" Marie-Claire protested.

"I did not say you were," Miss Podsnap told her. "You had plenty of time to remove my pearls from their box and take them away before anyone noticed that they were missing. You would not have had to take the box itself. I am very sorry to have troubled you. Miss Venn, can you give these young persons a small gratuity, for their time in assisting us with this matter?" Miss Venn distributed coins, and the maids left.

Miss Podsnap thought aloud: "Whoever took the pearls must have been in a hurry, otherwise why take the box, and not simply remove the pearls from it? M. Renard, are these rooms made up every day?"

"Indeed, Mademoiselle!" the manager cried out. "In other establishments, perhaps, the beds are not made up, but at the Grand National Hotel, the sheets are changed every other day, there is clean water available at all times, the *pots-de-chambre* are emptied daily. It is all very clean, very English." He leaned forward, conspiratorially. "I may inform you, Mademoiselle, that we will shortly be installing a lavatory on each floor, for use by all guests."

"How very, um, sanitary of you," Miss Podsnap said. "And I assume that all this is done on a strict schedule?"

M. Renard frowned. "That is the business of our housekeeper, of course, but we expect each of the rooms to be cleaned every day."

"Then whoever took the box must have been surprised by the servants who came in. This person must have opened the window and crept out onto the roof of the veranda, stayed there until the maids were finished, and then opened the window, got back into my room, and left through the corridor, just as any guest would do."

"One of our guests, a thief!" M. Renard was aghast. "Never!"

"Alas, quite probably," Miss Podsnap said. "Of course, no one knew exactly where the box was hidden, except you, Miss Venn. Or should I say, Miss Veneering?"

Miss Venn reddened in dismay. "What do you mean?"

"It's your nose, Miss Veneering. You have your father's colouring and form, but your mother had a most distinctive nose. I saw it many times, at those interminably dull dinner parties, and I wondered that she did not put a jewel in it, since she had hung them everywhere else upon her person. You could not have stolen the pearls yourself, since you were with me all morning, but you could have had an accomplice."

"I suppose I could have, but I didn't," Miss Venn retorted. "I didn't want the wretched things. Poor Mama is obsessed with what we lost. Sophronia was supposed to stay with her last night, but she sometimes takes a bit too much brandy at dinner. Mama must have followed me to the hotel last night. It will not happen again."

M. Renard fixed his eyes on Miss Venn. "This is insupportable, Madamoiselle! You must not let a mad woman range about the town at will, disturbing the guests at this hotel . . ."

"Mama is not mad!" Miss Venn cried out in despair. "She is not deranged, she is no danger to anyone, and she does not steal jewels! Sophronia looks after her well enough during the day, and last night was something of an exception. I cannot imagine why she should have taken so much brandy."

"It may be that you told her that I was here," Miss Podsnap said. "At one time, I thought Sophronia Lammle was my friend. I even offered to lend her money when she and her husband had to leave England. I should like to think that she regretted some of her actions, but it has been a very long time since I saw her, and she may have changed."

"This is of no importance," M. Renard said. "I must ask that this mad woman be confined!"

"No!" Miss Venn looked at Miss Podsnap. "I will not have Mama caged like some animal, put into a tub of water all day, under the care of nuns. She was insistent that I not be sent to a

Catholic convent school. And she did not come here this morning, because Sophronia was most contrite, and stayed with her all day."

"Besides," Miss Podsnap remarked, "it is highly unlikely that a woman of Mrs. Veneering's age and figure would perform acrobatics, such as getting in and out of windows, and standing for hours on the roof of a veranda. However, a young man might do so. I suggest a search of the rooms of Mr. George Magill, and possibly his mother and sister. They were in and out of several shops this morning, and it is possible that some of the merchandise that left with them was not strictly paid for in currency."

M. Renard rose with the light of battle in his eye. "Now I shall summon the police," he said. "The laws of France are not amenable to thieves, even though they are Americans." He bustled out, leaving the two English ladies to face each other.

Miss Podsnap spoke first. "I did not mean to disparage your mother," she said. "One cannot choose one's parents. Mine were quite dreadful, although I never said so to anyone except Sophronia."

"When did you realize that it was young Mr. Magill who had taken your pearls?" Miss Venn asked.

"Oh, it was quite obvious that he was not doing well at the Casino, and he was the only one who could have been in that corridor at that time of the day who knew that I had the pearls, and what I had done with them."

"But why on Earth did you dangle them so blatantly? It's as if you wanted them to be stolen!"

Miss Podsnap smiled ruefully. "I suppose I should tell you, now that this has been settled. Mr. Lightwood heard through other English friends who had stayed here that someone was stealing jewels from hotels in Deauville, and was worried that it was your Mama. I don't know whether it is because he thinks he has a debt to pay for all the meals he had at your parents' expense, or just because he is a lawyer and does not like to see someone prosecuted for a crime they did not commit, but he asked me to look into the matter when I came here. So I did. I've spent a lifetime watching people from the corners of the room; now I want to get into the room myself.

"Therefore, if you would care to accompany me on my travels, I can offer you a small emolument, which will allow Mrs. Veneering and Mrs. Lammle to live in seclusion, in some small place where they will not be tempted by the sight of English women wearing jewels."

"That is very kind of you," Miss Venn said.

"Besides," Miss Podsnap went on, "I think that when Mr. Magill tries to sell or pawn that necklace, he may get a nasty surprise. It is not as valuable as he thinks it is."

"Paste!" exclaimed Miss Venn.

"Let us say, a very good copy," Miss Podsnap corrected her. "People like the Magills should know better than to be taken in by appearances."

✗

THE ADVENTURE OF THE ELUSIVE EMERALDS

by Carla Coupe

Although these events occurred many years ago, I shall never forget the circumstances. For once, I played a rather dashing role, as the small gold locket on my watch chain constantly reminds me.

Our adventure began on a cold winter morning. A thick fog had rolled between the houses, and the windows opposite formed dark, shapeless blurs through the heavy yellow murk.

Inside, our gas lamps glowed bright and banished the gloom. As we breakfasted, Holmes quickly sorted through the usual pile of correspondence. After opening and reading several letters, he examined a small parcel that had arrived in the morning's post.

"Where is that from?" I asked.

"From Liverpool." A reminiscent smile touched his lips.

I repressed a shiver. My friend's heroic efforts to clear the reputation of a young Naval officer remained fresh in my mind, and I could not share Holmes's smile yet. Perhaps one day, after certain related events had faded from the public's memory, I would be permitted to tell that singular tale which had so nearly resulted in tragedy.

When opened, the parcel yielded a small jade dragon, exquisitely carved in the Oriental style. It was a lovely piece of work, a fitting token acknowledging the dangers Holmes had encountered and overcome.

After setting the dragon in pride of place upon the mantelpiece, Holmes buried himself in the most recent issue of the *Times*.

For the next hour or two, we sat on either side of the cheery fire, and only the rustle of the newspaper, the soft hiss of burning coal, and an occasional comment interrupted the quiet of our chambers. Shortly before eleven, Holmes rose and crossed to the window.

"Ah. Set aside your paper, Watson. I believe our caller has arrived."

"Are we expecting a visitor?" I placed the newspaper on an untidy pile and joined him at the window. In the street below, a brougham with a pair of matched greys waited at the kerb.

"This morning I received a note from Lord Maurice Denbeigh stating that he would call upon us at eleven. Would you look him up in Debretts?"

"Denbeigh?" I paused on my way to the bookshelf, then returned to the window. "I am familiar with the name. He's the second son of the Duke of Penfield. His Grace died five or six years ago, I believe, and Denbeigh's elder brother succeeded to the title."

"You are acquainted with the family?" Holmes glanced at me inquiringly.

"I met his mother, now the Dowager Duchess, at the Smythe-Parkinsons' a number of years ago. Fascinating woman."

I smiled, recalling that carefree time. Although the Smythe-Parkinsons were remote relatives, they had welcomed my visit.

A knock interrupted my reminiscences. At Holmes's nod, I hurried across the room and opened the door. Mrs Hudson entered, followed by a middle-aged man with fair hair and a colourless complexion.

"Lord Maurice Denbeigh," she said.

"Thank you, Mrs Hudson." I held the door for her as she left.

"How do you do," said Holmes. "I am Sherlock Holmes, and this is my associate, Doctor John Watson."

I bowed.

"Mr Holmes," Denbeigh burst out. "You must help me!"

Holmes gestured him to a chair. "I shall do my best. How can I assist you?"

He collapsed onto the chair like a man at the end of his strength. Holmes and I resumed our seats. Denbeigh buried his face in his hands for a moment, then raised his head and inhaled loudly.

"This is very difficult for me to speak of, gentlemen. It has to do with my mother, the Dowager Duchess of Penfield."

"I see." With a glance at me, Holmes crossed his legs and leaned back in his chair. "Pray continue."

"To put the problem in a nutshell, my brother, the present duke, is with his regiment in India. During his absence, all the responsibilities of the family have fallen upon my unhappy shoulders. For a year now, I've been driven nearly insane by my nephew, Hilary,

Viscount Sheppington. The boy is eighteen, and his escapades have caused me many a sleepless night. But now comes the crowning blow: My mother, my own mother, has turned thief."

"Her Grace a thief?" I could not conceal my outrage. "Oh come, sir, you must be mistaken!"

He stiffened. "Would I make such a shocking statement, Doctor, unless I was certain? I repeat, she is a thief, and a disgrace to our family."

Holmes raised an eyebrow. "I take it that monetary considerations are not involved?"

With a hollow laugh, Denbeigh sprang from his chair and paced the room.

"My mother has no concerns in that area, gentlemen." He paused before the fire, his head bowed. "Unlike others of us," he murmured.

"Then I can only assume that Her Grace is the victim of that unfortunate affliction known as kleptomania."

"Kleptomania?" I darted a glance at Holmes. "But the description of that illness has only recently been published. I take it you have been reading my French medical journals."

Holmes nodded once, his attention still upon Denbeigh.

"She *is* a kleptomaniac, Mr Holmes." He sighed, and despite his coat's fine tailoring, his shoulders bowed. "I spoke with several eminent nerve specialists, and they confirmed the shocking diagnosis. Not only are there the difficulties with shopkeepers to contend with; how can I explain to friends of the family when Mother decides to pocket some valuable memento whilst paying calls?"

"A vexing problem, indeed," replied Holmes.

"And though it is petty thefts today, how can I be certain she won't lapse into more serious criminality? Mr Holmes, you must help me find some way out of this intolerable situation. For the family's sake, I am willing to pay—"

A loud series of knocks came from the front of the house. Denbeigh started nervously and glanced about.

The rich, husky voice of a woman rose above Mrs Hudson's gentle murmurs.

"Mother!" cried Denbeigh.

At the sound of rapidly approaching footsteps, we rose and faced the door.

After a single knock, it opened, revealing Mrs Hudson again. She only had time to say, "Her Grace, the Dowager Duchess of Penfield," before the lady swept past her into our chambers.

Beneath an elegant feathered hat, her chestnut hair was now streaked with silver, yet she looked every inch the magnificent woman I remembered. She dismissed Mrs Hudson, then glanced from me to Holmes.

"Which of you gentlemen is Mr Sherlock Holmes?"

Holmes stepped forward. "I am."

She held out her hand, and he took it, bowing low.

Straightening, Holmes released her hand. "And this is my friend and colleague, Doctor John Watson. I believe you have met before."

"Oh?" She fixed me with sparkling, dark eyes. "Where was that, Doctor?"

"Several years ago, at the Smythe-Parkinsons'."

"Charming people," she said with a small smile and a gracious nod. "They always host the most amusing parties."

"Yes, indeed, Your Grace." I was a trifle disappointed that she did not appear to remember me, but why should a duchess remember a simple military doctor?

"Maurice," she said, transferring her gaze to her son. He flinched, and she let out a little sigh. "I thought I had made my wishes clear."

His waxen cheeks took on a rosy tinge, and he shifted in place as if he were a schoolboy.

"You had, Mother. However, I thought—"

"I'm certain you did." She walked to the door and opened it. "We shall discuss this further in private, Maurice. You may kiss me before you go."

She tilted her head, presenting her cheek. Denbeigh glanced at Holmes, who bowed.

"Your Lordship."

"Goodbye, Mr Holmes. Doctor."

Denbeigh crossed to the duchess, obediently kissed her cheek, and left. I closed the door behind him and turned, my attention captured by Her Grace's elegant form.

"Gentlemen, I fear my son has placed me in an invidious position." She crossed to the fireplace and examined the assortment of items displayed on the mantelpiece. When her gaze lit upon the tobacco-filled slipper, she smiled.

"How so?" Holmes enquired, standing beside the settee.

"He has been spreading dreadful rumours about me." She moved around the room, casting a cool glance over the well-worn furnishings. At least Mrs Hudson had tidied yesterday, although Her Grace didn't appear distressed by our usual clutter. I was grateful that Holmes had not conducted any chemical experiments recently, for they often filled the room with smoke and an appalling stench: an altogether unsuitable atmosphere in which to receive a dowager duchess.

Holmes's intelligent gaze followed her perambulations.

"What sort of rumours?" he asked.

Her Grace turned to Holmes with a frown.

"Pray, do not play coy with me, Mr Holmes. Maurice believes I am suffering from some sort of nervous disorder and is, I am certain, preparing to have me declared incompetent." She raised a gloved hand to her bosom.

"Gracious me," I said, appalled. I hurried over to her. "What a shocking—"

"Thank you, Doctor, but I do not require sympathy." She lifted her chin and gazed solemnly at Holmes.

"These are indeed serious charges," said Holmes.

"They are." She hesitated for a moment, indecision briefly written upon her face. Then she stepped to my side and rested her hand on my arm. Her fingers trembled.

"As much as I find discussing my personal circumstances distasteful, it appears to be necessary," she said, her voice low. "Gentlemen, I control my personal fortune outright. My son's expenses have far exceeded his income, and although I have settled some of his debts, he continues to ask for more money." She glanced from me to Holmes. "You understand the advantages to him were my finances to be under his control."

Holmes nodded.

"Yes, of course," I replied, and ventured to rest my hand upon hers for a moment.

"Thank you." She smiled and gave my arm a gentle squeeze. "Anything you can do to dispel the rumours would be a great

service to me. Otherwise, we shall speak no more of this matter."
She swept to the door.

"I will see you out," I said, hurrying to open it.

She paused in the entrance hall, drawing on her gloves, and gazed at me for a moment.

"The Smythe-Parkinsons, you say?"

I smoothed my rumpled jacket. "Yes, Your Grace. At a fancy-dress ball."

"Ah, that explains my lapse of memory," she replied with a nod. "After all, is not concealment the very point of fancy dress?"

"Of course." Although it was clear she still did not remember me, at least she was gracious enough to provide an excuse.

I helped her to her carriage, then returned to our chambers.

"What a superb woman." I closed the door behind me and took my seat.

Holmes chuckled and walked to the fireplace, his pipe in hand. "Yes, quite remarkable, isn't she?"

"Luckily we weren't taken in by Denbeigh's story."

After leaning to light a twist of paper in the fireplace, Holmes straightened, lit his pipe, and waited until it was drawing properly before replying.

"You recall that jade dragon I received in this morning's post?"

"Yes, you put it on the mantelpiece." I looked up and gasped. "Good Lord, it has vanished!"

"Precisely." Holmes's voice was filled with satisfaction. "Either Her Grace is so brilliant a kleptomaniac that she has achieved an unnoticed theft at 221B Baker Street or her son wishes us to think so."

"Well, of all the amazing nerve!"

"Watson, we have met a worthy antagonist." Holmes suddenly emptied his pipe into the fire and strode to the door. "Come along, old chap. Don your hat and coat. I think we will take the liberty of providing the duchess with an unobtrusive escort."

The streetlamps glowed warmly as I limped after Holmes into Carrington's, the silversmiths on Regent Street.

"Holmes, this is the twelfth shop we've visited," I whispered. "My feet are tired, my leg aches. We've been following the duchess all afternoon."

"I was eager to observe Her Grace amongst temptation." Holmes hovered by a display case.

"Temptation?" I grumbled. "As far as I can see, she hasn't been tempted to do anything except purchase a variety of items in far too many shops."

"Well, I must admit that I have not observed any untoward behaviour thus far," Holmes replied.

Across the shop, the duchess studied a display of small silver goods laid out upon the counter. The manager, a tall, lugubrious Scot with an unfortunate squint, hovered over her like a stork over a new-born chick as she examined piece after piece.

The door bell rang, and a fashionably dressed young man with curling, chestnut hair stepped inside the shop.

"Hullo, Grandmama!" he called, waving his stick. "Saw the carriage outside and thought you might be here."

Her Grace turned and regarded the young man with a fond smile.

"Ah, Hilary. I wondered when you would find me." Turning to face us, she continued. "Mr Holmes, Doctor. Do stop trying to disappear into the woodwork and come meet my grandson."

Holmes and I exchanged a glance. Warmth spread across my cheeks, but Holmes appeared amused.

Introductions were quickly made. Her Grace returned to her examination of silver toothpick holders and other small trinkets, while the viscount eyed the items on the counter and criticised each one. He then stepped to my side and nudged me with an elbow.

"Keeping an eye on Grandmama, eh? Capital idea. My uncle informed me that he intended to consult you regarding her condition," he whispered. "Can't be too careful when she's out and about."

"I beg your pardon," I replied, drawing away. What effrontery!

"Not at all." He winked, returning to Her Grace when she called to him.

The duchess completed her purchase. A smile touched her lips as she turned to Holmes.

"I am returning home now, Mr Holmes. You are released from duty."

Holmes barked a laugh and then bowed.

"Your Grace is too kind."

She then gestured to me. "Doctor, accompany me to my carriage, if you please."

I was delighted to offer this small service and gave her my arm. We were followed by a shop assistant carrying her parcel.

As I handed her into her carriage, the viscount hurried from the shop. "I say, Grandmama! I may as well return home with you."

He brushed past me and climbed into the carriage.

I waited until the brougham had clattered down the street and turned the corner before re-entering the shop. Holmes was deep in conversation with the manager.

"Ah, Watson," he said as I approached. "Mr Ferguson has a question for you."

Mr Ferguson leaned across the counter. "Doctor, did you see Her Grace pick up a wee enameled card case? The green one?" he asked, his voice a murmur.

I thought for a moment before replying in the same soft tones.

"I believe Her Grace examined one, but I'm certain she returned it to the counter. Why?"

"A card case has gone missing," said Holmes, looking unruffled. "Although before searching any further, Mr Ferguson, I would ask Watson to show us the contents of his left outer pocket."

"The contents of my . . ." I stared at Holmes as I slipped my hand into the pocket. "Why, there is nothing—Good Lord!"

I drew out my hand. A small green card case rested in my palm.

Ferguson uttered a strangled sound and reached for the case.

"But I never touched it," I cried, allowing Ferguson to snatch it away. "How could it—?"

"Calm yourself, my dear fellow," said Holmes, clapping a hand on my shoulder. "No one believes you were responsible for taking it."

"I should hope not!"

"No, it appears she took it from the counter and then slipped it into your pocket."

"But Holmes, the viscount could have—"

Holmes squeezed my shoulder and gave an almost imperceptible shake of his head. He turned to Ferguson. "I believe you have heard rumours about Her Grace, Mr Ferguson."

I could hardly believe my ears. Holmes was as good as stating that the duchess was responsible for the theft. Surely the viscount had the same opportunity to take the card case and slip it into my pocket as his grandmother.

"Aye, I have." Ferguson sighed. "Though I thought to pay them no heed."

"It is a sad case," Holmes said softly. "And one that, were it made public, could bring shame upon the family."

"But what am I to do if it happens again, Mr Holmes?" Ferguson asked, frowning. "She frequently patronises our business. I cannae call the police, but the losses—"

"I believe I have a solution to your problem." Holmes smiled. "Observe her whenever she visits. Anything that is not paid for should be added to her account. I believe this will prove most satisfactory for both parties in handling any such incidents in the future."

Ferguson's dour expression cleared. "That would suit us quite well, Mr Holmes."

"Excellent," said Holmes. "In that way your shop will sustain no loss, and the family will be spared public scandal. Yes, a very satisfactory arrangement, I think." He turned to me. "Come along, Watson."

I could barely wait until we were out of the shop and walking along the pavement before turning to Holmes.

"But, Holmes! Her Grace might not be guilty; the viscount could have as easily taken the card case."

"I know that, dear fellow," he said, raising his stick toward an unoccupied hansom. The driver reined in the horse. "Did you notice that she appeared very fond of the boy?"

"I did indeed. Yet that does not explain why you have cast suspicion solely upon her."

After giving our address, Holmes and I climbed inside the cab.

"Watson, I am in the process of setting a trap." Holmes signaled with his stick, and the driver set off. "I have deep reservations regarding Sheppington. He may be using his grandmother's regard for him and playing upon her affections, either alone or in collusion with his uncle. If Denbeigh and Sheppington are guilty of conspiring in order to gain control of Her Grace's fortune, I will draw them out and expose their machinations."

"So you believe her to be the victim of a plot?"

"Possibly, Watson, possibly. If, on the other hand, she does suffer from kleptomania, we must see to it that she does not have the opportunity to disgrace herself and her family by being publicly exposed."

"But how are we to do that?"

"We took the first step this afternoon. Our next task is to send a message and ask Denbeigh and Sheppington to call upon us on the morrow."

The next day dawned bright and chill. Holmes and I were immersed in the morning newspapers and Mrs Hudson was clearing our breakfast dishes when the bell announced visitors. She bustled out with a tray of crockery, only to appear again moments later, breathing heavily.

"Her Grace," she panted.

The dowager duchess entered, heavily veiled. With a brisk nod, Her Grace dismissed Mrs Hudson, then lifted the veils before turning to Holmes.

"Mr Holmes, Doctor. I apologise for calling unannounced."

She appeared slightly flustered, but when I suggested she be seated, she gave an impatient wave.

"No time, gentlemen. I overheard Maurice speaking of his visit; he will be here soon."

"How may we be of assistance?" asked Holmes.

"Count von Kratzov is giving a ball tomorrow. He currently occupies one of my properties in Town; therefore I must make an appearance." She paced from the hearth to the breakfast table and back. "He will be displaying the von Kratzov emeralds, the first time they have been publicly shown outside of Poland. I suspect that Maurice may attempt some mischief in order to disgrace me and further his aims."

"We must prevent that from occurring, Holmes!" I said.

"Indeed we must." Holmes looked inquiringly at her. "Would it be possible to procure an invitation for the good doctor and me?"

"I would be grateful if you and Doctor Watson would accompany me."

Holmes shook his head. "It would be best if we were not of your party."

"Ah. Of course." She smiled. "I will drop a hint to a friend, who will ensure that you both are included on the list of guests." She held out her hand to Holmes, who bowed over it briefly.

"Excellent!" Holmes glanced at the clock. "And now I am expecting your son—"

"Yes!" She lowered her veils and hurried to the door. "Thank you, Mr Holmes, Doctor."

Rather than bother Mrs Hudson, I saw Her Grace to the pavement and hailed a hansom for her. She thanked me most prettily before departing.

I had barely gained our chambers before the bell rang again. Within moments, Denbeigh entered, accompanied by his nephew.

I bowed, but remained in my place by the window where I could clearly see both men. If either Denbeigh or Sheppington attempted to surreptitiously pocket an item in order to dishonour Her Grace, I wished to be the one who revealed their perfidy.

As Holmes explained the advantages of forging agreements with all of the shops patronised by Her Grace, Sheppington prowled about the room before lounging against the hearth. He withdrew a silver case from his pocket, extracted a cigarette, and lit it.

Denbeigh frowned. "And what is to prevent these shopkeepers from falsely charging my mother for items she did not take?"

"These are the most reputable establishments in London," said Holmes. "Any such allegations would be ruinous."

"I agree with Mr Holmes, Uncle." The young man shrugged and flicked his half-smoked cigarette into the embers. "If we can't stop Grandmama pinching the stuff, at least this will keep it quiet."

"Hilary!" Denbeigh appeared scandalised. He turned to my friend. "Very well, Mr Holmes. Although I have reservations, we shall try your suggestion."

Holmes coughed gently. "Matters are already arranged at Carrington's. All that remains to be done is to make similar agreements with the other shops your mother patronises. Would you care for me to undertake this task?"

"That won't be necessary, Mr Holmes," said Denbeigh stiffly. "I shall take responsibility for this matter myself."

Dropping onto a chair, Sheppington crossed his legs at the ankle and leaned back. "I only wish that since Grandmama's so free and easy with other people's belongings, she'd loosen up the money bags for me a little. I'm stone broke. And Uncle, I know you've lost a bundle—"

"We will not discuss that at present, Hilary." Denbeigh glanced at Holmes. "Do you have further advice regarding my mother's affliction?"

"Not at present."

"Then we shall bid you good day. Come, Hilary."

Sheppington heaved a sigh as he rose. "Of course. Goodbye, Mr Holmes, Doctor Watson."

Holmes turned to the window, while I saw His Lordship and his nephew to the door.

"Do you believe Denbeigh will follow your suggestion and contact the shopkeepers?" I returned to my chair. "He did not seem especially taken with the idea."

"Very true. You noticed that he did not mention the ball or the emeralds?"

"Why would—" I stopped, suddenly struck by Holmes's implication. "Do you believe that omission to be suspicious?"

"Possibly so." Holmes's shrug was positively Gallic. "Another possibility exits, however. If Denbeigh knows the emeralds are well protected, and that his mother would have little chance to pilfer them, he would have no cause for concern."

"So, we shall spend tomorrow evening observing Her Grace," I said. "I can only hope it is less arduous than our afternoon trailing her about the shops."

"I suspect that observing Her Grace will be the least interesting portion of our evening," said Holmes with a laugh.

"What do you mean?"

"You heard Her Grace, Watson. This will be the first time the von Kratzov emeralds will be on display outside Poland, and not only will they be an object of interest to members of society, but they will attract the attention of every jewel thief in Europe."

"Good God, do you think so?"

"I do indeed." Holmes's eyes sparkled. "In fact, I will be very much surprised if we do not encounter several notorious thieves during the course of the evening."

"But Holmes! Should we not inform Scotland Yard of your suspicions?"

"I am certain that the count has taken every precaution," he replied. "But it is a clear day, if a trifle chill. I suggest we take the air now, for I shall be occupied later this afternoon."

I rose and followed him. We donned our coats and gloves, and as we stepped onto the pavement, Holmes reached into his pocket and froze.

"Holmes!" I exclaimed, gazing at his countenance in alarm. "What is wrong? Are you ill?"

He took a deep, shuddering breath, threw his head back, and emitted a bark of laughter that would have frightened me if he hadn't immediately calmed.

"I am well, Watson." His dark eyes flashed as he withdrew his hand from his pocket. He opened his fingers, and laying on the kidskin was the jade dragon.

"Bless me!" I stared at the bauble.

"Indeed." Holmes chuckled and returned the dragon to his pocket. "This is becoming quite a pretty puzzle, my dear chap. Who is returning the stolen articles? The thief, for some unknown reason? Or another party who wishes to prevent a scandal?" He clapped on his hat. "Come, Watson."

I followed him, still overcome with astonishment. If Holmes was correct regarding the interest generated by the jewels, as he almost invariably was about these things, tomorrow evening would test our abilities. The combination of the finest emeralds in Europe and Her Grace could only mean trouble.

After luncheon, Holmes remarked that he would be absent from our chambers for some time, since he would be occupied with certain investigations.

I spent a quiet afternoon and evening alone, perusing the newspapers and other publications for any hint of gossip or innuendo regarding Her Grace and her family. Apart from His Lordship frequenting the races, however, they garnered no mention in the press.

I was not unduly concerned by Holmes's absence; he occasionally disappeared for hours or days at a time when immersed in an investigation. He did not return to our chambers that night, or if he had, he arrived late and departed before I awoke. Our invitations to Count von Kratzov's ball that evening arrived before luncheon; however, I had seen nothing of Holmes throughout the day, nor received word of his whereabouts.

The sky was darkening into dusk when I rose to dress. I glanced at the clock; Holmes was deucedly late. Had he forgotten our promise to Her Grace and Lord Maurice to attend the ball?

At that moment, a flurry of knocks sounded from the front door, followed by raised voices. My chamber door was flung open, and a man dressed in soiled work clothes, clutching a flat cap hurried in, followed by Mrs Hudson.

"Oh, Doctor!" she cried. "He would not wait—"

"I should hope not." The man spoke with familiar voice. "Thank you, Mrs Hudson."

I started. "Holmes?"

With a sigh, Mrs Hudson left. Holmes removed the putty that had altered the contours of his nose and smiled.

"Good afternoon, Watson. I hope you are preparing to dress for—"

"Really, Holmes." I gazed at his grimy clothing and shook my head. "You are absolutely disgusting."

"My dear fellow, the disguise was necessary," he said, eyes twinkling. "It enabled me to acquire information regarding Her Grace. Let us change our clothing, and I shall tell you in the cab on the way to Count von Kratzov's."

The evening gloom had fallen by the time we finished dressing and descended the stair. Mrs Hudson stood before the door, holding Holmes's hat.

"I have brushed it as best I can, Mr Holmes," she said, as he donned his coat and scarf and pulled on his gloves. "I really don't know how you manage to get so filthy."

"As I said at the time, it was not my fault, Mrs Hudson. Blame Red O'Toole, the bare knuckle fighter, and his propensity for taking offense at gentlemen in evening clothes." She shook her head as Holmes took his hat. Clapping it on, he smiled and chose his stick. "Excellent!"

I turned away and suppressed my smile.

"Thank you, Mrs Hudson," I said, buttoning my coat and drawing on my gloves before taking up my own hat and stick.

I followed Holmes into the bustling crowds, for despite the chill, the streets teemed with activity. Holmes hailed a hansom and after giving the count's Grosvenor Place address to the driver, he sat back on the leather seat with a small sigh.

"You asked about my activities today," Holmes began. "You will be pleased to know I performed honest labour and a little reconnaissance. With the assistance of Mary, the youngest and most imaginative of Her Grace's housemaids, I repaired several broken panes in Her Grace's dressing room."

I glanced at Holmes. "How convenient that there were broken panes which required repair."

He did not reply, but simply flashed a small smile and folded his hands upon his knee.

"And how were those panes broken?" I continued. "Your young colleagues throwing rocks, perhaps?"

"It is positively shameful how these hooligans run wild."

I was not at all surprised Holmes had arranged such an event. In the interests of justice, he maintained that to prove the greater crime, one could be forgiven the lesser. I generally agreed.

"And what about young Mary?" I turned a critical eye on him. "I hope you did not play upon her expectations."

"Never fear, my dear fellow. I assure you that our relations were entirely proper. Her eldest brother is a glazier in Plymouth, and we spoke of the demands of his trade after the fleet has returned to port." He lifted an eyebrow. "You would be surprised at the amount of destruction perpetrated by Her Majesty's forces whilst in their cups."

"I assure you, I would not." I suppressed vivid memories of the actions of my military brethren during leave. "And what news did Mary convey?"

"A great deal of commiseration for Her Grace and Lord Maurice regarding the activities of Viscount Sheppington, some of which were conveyed in a whisper, with hints of others that were far worse and could not be spoken of."

I shook my head. "Is the young man truly so far sunk in vice and dissipation?"

"Apparently so, although when I enquired if she had witnessed any of his dreadful behaviour, she denied it."

"Then how did she know of it?"

"Ah, there's the question, Watson. Rumour amongst the other servants is the most likely cause; however, I have identified a few other possibilities."

Before I could ask him to elaborate, our cab came to a halt.

"Number sixteen, sir," said the driver.

As Holmes paid, I wrapped my scarf closer around my neck and stepped to the pavement amidst the confusion of a dozen cabs and carriages disgorging their passengers.

The count's house sat at the end of the row, brightly lit windows facing both Grosvenor Place and the side street. The façade was of fine Portland stone with elaborately carved lintels. A heavy granite wall bordered the pavement, leaving the narrow well between wall and house immersed in a pool of black. During the day, those subterranean rooms whose windows faced the wall would receive scant illumination; at night, the darkness was Stygian.

Gentlemen and ladies hurried by and quickly mounted the steps. The open front door welcomed guests as the music from within wafted to the street.

"This should prove an entertaining evening, Watson." Holmes joined me on the pavement. "I have already spotted one jewel thief in the crowd, and there may very well be more."

I turned to stare at the passersby. "So your suspicions were correct! What dreadful news!"

"Calm yourself, my dear fellow. Come, let us join the others and see the legendary emeralds for ourselves."

We were ushered inside and shortly thereafter presented to the Count von Kratzov, a portly little man with eyes as black and round as shoe buttons.

"Welcome, Mr Holmes, Dr Watson." He spoke perfect English, despite a heavy accent. "Your reputation precedes you, Mr Holmes. Should I be concerned about the safety of my jewels?"

Holmes bowed. "That depends upon the security of your arrangements."

"Ah, of course. You shall judge for yourself." He glanced at a thin, sharp-featured man with the stooped shoulders of a scholar who stood to one side, and addressed him in what I assumed to be Polish. "My private secretary will accompany us."

Excusing himself from his other guests, the count led us down the corridor toward the rear of the house to a receiving room where a burly footman stood beside a door. The count drew out a key hanging on his watch fob, unlocked the door, and preceded us into a small drawing room. A glass case rested atop the polished mahogany table. On the other side of the room sat a broad fireplace. The hearth was cold, and the chamber's sole illumination came from a gas fixture arranged to shed its light upon the table, leaving the rest of the room in shadow. Once inside, the count closed and relocked the door and then gestured toward the closed windows that faced Chapel Street. Through the glass, I could see closely spaced iron bars.

"This door is the only means of entering or exiting this room, gentlemen, and I myself hold the sole key. Only a few select guests will be invited to view the stones, but in case anyone tries to slip in unobserved, Stanislaw is on guard outside. He has served my family for many years and is completely trustworthy." The count lifted his eyebrows and looked at Holmes. "As you can see, I have taken every precaution."

Holmes studied the room for a moment. "Your secretary does not have a duplicate key?" he asked.

The count chuckled and turned to the man who stood as still as a statue just inside the door. "Carolus, explain please."

Carolus gently cleared his throat. "This morning, before we brought the jewels from the bank where they had been housed for safekeeping, I oversaw the installation of a new lock on the door. The locksmith himself handed the only key to my master."

"I see." Holmes turned to the glittering gems, nestled on black velvet inside the case.

I leaned forward. The emeralds were magnificent, with brilliant colour and unparalleled clarity. There were eight stones in all, each cut in a different style and displayed in an elegant setting, save for the largest and most spectacular stone. It lay in the center of the case, loose and unadorned; it needed no other device to enhance its beauty.

Holmes nodded once, and we followed the count into the corridor.

"I commend you on your arrangements," said Holmes, as the count closed and locked the drawing room door. Carolus bowed and slipped away.

The count smiled and rubbed his hands together. "Your words comfort me, Mr Holmes. And now, shall we join my other guests?"

As we entered the ballroom, an elderly matron approached and playfully batted the count's arm with her fan.

"Count! You have been avoiding me!" she said as she neatly separated von Kratzen from Holmes, much as a dog would separate a lamb from the flock. They disappeared into the crush, and I turned to Holmes.

"Well, Holmes, the count has certainly established a secure location for the stones. I cannot see how anyone could steal them."

"I wish that were the case." He glanced at me, then clasped his hands behind his back and turned to contemplate the dancing couples moving about the floor. "I have identified five possible methods for surreptitiously removing one or more of the emeralds from their case and then from the room. I am certain, were I to exert myself, I could add half-a-dozen more."

"Surely you jest!" I stared at Holmes in surprise. "The door is locked, the windows are closed and barred, and a guard is stationed outside. What more could be done?"

"What more, indeed." A smile touched the corners of his mouth. "If all my adversaries were as straightforward as you, I would have no fears at all about the fate of the von Kratzov emeralds."

His words stung. "If my contributions are so useless, I wonder that you include me in your investigations at all." I accepted a glass of champagne from a passing footman and drank rather more deeply than usual.

"Watson!" Holmes turned to me, his brows drawn together, yet not in a scowl. "I beg your pardon, my dear fellow. My words were ill chosen. Do not ask me, however, to apologise for the sentiment. Your mind acts as a touchstone to that which is pure and good; although agile, it lacks the sordid depths and devious paths of the criminal's mental processes."

Somewhat comforted, I took another sip of the count's excellent champagne.

"What would you have me do this evening?" I asked.

"Will you assume responsibility for following Her Grace? I shall concern myself with observing Denbeigh and Sheppington."

"With pleasure. But do you think it possible that she could steal one or more of the emeralds and elude detection?"

"That, of course, is the crux of the matter, isn't it?" With an enigmatic smile, Holmes disappeared into the crowd.

A few moments later, Her Grace was announced, along with her son and grandson. I could see no sign of Holmes, yet I had no doubt he knew the whereabouts of every individual in the room.

Mindful of my charge, I peered at the dowager duchess and her party over the rim of my champagne flute. Resplendent in diamonds and sapphires, Her Grace displayed an engaging vivacity. She smiled at the count's attentions, which were so marked as to be offensively Continental; indeed he stood so close that he actually trod upon her skirts. With a thunderous expression, Sheppington clenched his hands into fists, but a word from Denbeigh stilled him. Drawing the young man away with a firm hand upon his shoulder, Denbeigh led him toward the supper room.

Her Grace continued to smile as the count gestured and spoke, yet her gaze appeared to follow their retreating forms. It was only upon the announcement of the arrival of another guest that the count bowed and turned away, leaving the duchess alone.

I stepped forward and, catching her eye, bowed.

She approached and extended her hand. "So here you are, Doctor."

I raised her hand to my lips and then, somewhat reluctantly I confess, released it.

Leaning close, she lowered her voice. "I assume Mr Holmes is also here?"

"He is, Your Grace."

She nodded in abstraction. A young guardsman inadvertently jostled her, and after politely receiving his incoherent apology, she drew a deep breath and took my arm in a firm clasp.

"Let us remove ourselves from the throng," she said. I led her to a quiet corner by a heavily curtained window, and she continued: "You mentioned that we had met before at the Smythe-Parkinsons'."

"Yes, several years ago. At a fancy dress ball." I smiled at the memory of that carefree country weekend.

"What were you wearing?"

"I went as Pierrot. Not very original, I am afraid," I said, my face warming. A more elaborate costume had been beyond my means.

"I am certain you looked most handsome." The duchess tilted her head inquiringly. "And do you remember what I wore?"

"Of course. An Elizabethan-inspired dress in blue," I replied promptly. "I believe it was velvet. You were enchanting."

Indeed, she had outshone women half her age. No one attending the ball that night could have failed to admire her verve and beauty. Even now, so many years later, I picture her clearly.

"Ah, yes. That costume did suit me rather well, did it not?" She smiled and pressed my arm. "I am flattered you remembered me."

"You were impossible to forget."

"Doctor, you missed your true calling," she said with a laugh. "You are quite the diplomat."

At that moment, the count appeared before us, flanked by the dowager duchess's son and grandson. I could not help but see the trio as examples of the worst traits of modern man: Count von Kratzov, coarse beneath his veneer of urbanity; Lord Maurice, colourless and cowed, living his life in a perpetual state of nervous exhaustion; and Viscount Sheppington, whose youthful attractiveness hid, by many accounts, a dissolute character.

"Doctor Watson!" Denbeigh appeared startled. "I did not expect to see you here. Is Mr Holmes also in attendance?"

"Yes, he's about," I said. "We were pleased to accept Count von Kratzov's invitation."

"The pleasure is all mine," said the count before turning to the dowager duchess. "Your Grace, I would be honoured if you would give me the next dance."

She sighed, the exhalation so soft I am certain I alone heard it. With a final squeeze, she released my arm and turned to the men.

"Thank you, Count von Kratzov. However, I am a trifle fatigued. Might I prevail upon you to show me those magnificent emeralds instead?"

For a moment the tableau stilled, as if each player were frozen in time. Even the music paused, and during that short-lived quiet, I heard a soft, sharp inhalation, although I could not tell from whom it issued. Then a woman's shrill laugh rang through the room, and the silence ended as suddenly as it had begun, movement and sound resuming.

The count's expression briefly darkened, then his scowl disappeared as quickly as it had come.

"But of course, dear lady," he said, bowing and offering his arm.

The dowager duchess hesitated only a heartbeat before resting her gloved hand upon his. She glanced at me over her shoulder, and I do not believe I mistook the plea in her gaze.

"Doctor, you will join us, won't you?"

"It would be my very great pleasure, Your Grace."

Von Kratzov escorted her across the room. Denbeigh and I followed in their wake, as cygnets paddle behind a swan. The four of us had gained the receiving room, and I saw that Stanislaw still stood guard before the door. Denbeigh plucked at my sleeve.

"Doctor, a word, if you please."

The count ushered the dowager duchess into the small room that housed the emeralds as I turned to Denbeigh.

"Her Grace asked me to . . ." I began. Stanislaw closed the door and turned to face us, his broad Slavic features impassive.

Denbeigh's grip tightened and he pulled me to the far side of the room. "I will only take a moment."

"A moment, then." I glanced at the drawing room's closed door.

Leaning close, Denbeigh spoke low. "Where is Mr Holmes?"

"As I said before, he is somewhere about."

"But why is he not here, observing my mother?" His fingers dug into my arm.

"You must ask Holmes yourself. I cannot speak for his actions." I pulled from his grasp and stepped away.

"Of course not," he said, the colour high on his cheeks. "Forgive me, I am simply concerned about my mother."

"I understand," I replied, my irritation fading. "Holmes and I both share your concern, and I am certain that, whatever he is doing, he is endeavouring to prevent any incidents from occurring that would involve Her Grace. Now, if you will excuse—"

"One more question, please, Doctor." He waited until I nodded before continuing. "Do you think it significant that she asked to see the emeralds?"

"Not at all. They are unparalleled in Europe and justifiably famous. I would think it odd if she did not."

Before he could respond, a shriek pierced the air, followed by heavy thuds and a sharp crack, then the sound of shattering glass.

I whirled toward the closed door. "Good God, what is that!"

My exclamation overlay Denbeigh's cry of "Mother!" We dashed to where Stanislaw, startled from his impassivity, pulled upon the door handle without effect.

"Locked!" he grunted.

I motioned him away.

"Your Grace! Your Grace, can you hear me?" I pounded upon the heavy oak with my fist, then pressed my ear against the panels. My heart sank at the silence within. What could have happened to her?

Suffused with anger at myself, I bit back my curses. I had failed in my duty; I should have ignored Denbeigh's request and attended her! I raised my fist, raining blows upon the panels.

"Watson!" From seemingly out of the æther, Holmes appeared at my side.

"Her Grace may be in danger!" I cried, continuing my battery upon the door.

"She and the count are within?" His quicksilver intellect grasped the situation immediately. "Do not blame yourself, Watson," he said, drawing me away.

With a glance and a nod at Stanislaw, Holmes doffed his coat and handed it to me.

Denbeigh raised his hands in supplication. "Do something, Mr Holmes!"

Holmes's expression hardened. "Stand back," he ordered.

Upon a word from Holmes, he and Stanislaw pressed their shoulders to the oak. The wood creaked, but did not give. They tried again with the same result.

The room grew crowded with the concerned and curious, and I instructed several footmen to encourage the onlookers to return to the ballroom, or at least to keep clear a space for Holmes and Stanislaw.

They hurled themselves against the door again. With a loud crack, the latch at last gave. Thrusting Stanislaw to one side,

Holmes darted into the dark room. I followed, ignoring Denbeigh's breathless cries and clutching fingers.

For a moment, sufficient illumination spilled across the threshold to show the overturned table. Before I could discern further details, Denbeigh and Stanislaw crowded the doorway, blocking the brightness.

"Let no one else enter!" ordered Holmes.

Stanislaw turned to face the outer room, a more effective barricade than the violated door.

"Take care, Watson!" Holmes's voice came from across the room. "Let me light the lamp before you venture further."

Although wild with concern for Her Grace's safety, I saw the sense of his request and followed his bidding. He struck a Lucifer and the small flame flared in the darkness, sending dreadful shadows dancing across the walls and illuminating Holmes's grim expression. He stepped to the fixture, and in the still room I could briefly hear the hiss of gas before the sudden burst of light caused me to shade my eyes.

Blinking as I adjusted to the light, I needed only a single glance to take in the room's utter confusion. As I had observed earlier, the table was tipped on its side, the legs facing the open door. The glass case containing the emeralds lay overturned on the floor by the fireplace. Curtains, now torn, sagged, and light glittered off the shards of several smashed window panes.

A soft moan startled me. I turned to the window, my breath catching: There, half-hidden by a swath of damask pulled from its hanger, lay the dowager duchess.

"Good God!"

In an instant I knelt beside her, gently lifting her limp, ungloved hand. Her pulse, weak and thready, strengthened as she stirred. Minute pieces of glass glistened in her hair and upon her bodice.

"Do not attempt to move," I said, carefully touching her temple, then lifting my hand to the light. Blood, dark and viscous, stained my fingertips.

She groaned, then appeared to slip back into unconsciousness.

"Holmes, she is in need of immediate assistance."

Holmes bent over the far end of the table, which almost touched the opposite wall. He grasped one corner and tugged it from the wall.

"I fear she is not the only one," he said, his voice grave. "Count? Count von Kratzov? Can you hear me?"

I reluctantly released her hand and stood. My medical vows required me to ascertain the count's condition, although I was still concerned about the dowager duchess. I walked to Holmes's side and gasped. The count lay sprawled in the corner, his face and shirt-front spattered with blood. I bent over him and rested my fingers on his pulse.

A sudden commotion at the door drew my attention.

"Grandmama! Grandmama!" Sheppington cried. "Let me through, you rogue!"

A scuffle ensued at the door, ending only when the young man dodged beneath Stanislaw's outstretched arm and darted into the room. His wild gaze roamed over Holmes and me, coming to rest upon the form of the dowager duchess.

Falling to his knees before his grandmother, he caught her hand in his.

"I am too late! The count has killed her!" He choked back a sob.

"Pull yourself together," said Holmes. Bent over from the waist, he was carefully examining the ruined jewel case on the floor beside the fireplace. A rough circle of shards and patches of glass ground to powder glinted upon the carpet and planks. "She is nowhere near death."

"Do not move her yet," I said, turning back to my patient. "Holmes, I require more light."

"Maryja, matka Boga!"

I glanced up. Carolus entered the room, carrying an oil lamp.

"Bring the lamp here," I ordered, loosening the count's cravat.

He placed the lamp on the floor beside me, then clasped his hands behind his back.

"What has happened? Who has done this to my master?" he asked.

"That is what we are trying to ascertain," replied Holmes. He picked up the shattered jewel case and held it to the light.

Carolus gasped. "The emeralds!"

I finished my examination of the count, then rose stiffly, retrieving the lamp.

"The count has been badly beaten and appears to have fallen and struck his head, resulting in his current state of unconsciousness.

However, I do not believe he has any broken bones, nor any internal injuries." I turned to Carolus. "Have two or three of your strongest footmen carry him to his bed. Does he have a private physician?"

"Yes. He consults Sir Theobald Western, of Harley Street. Sir Theobald is in attendance tonight."

"Excellent. Send a footman to find him and take him to the count."

The dowager duchess stirred, groaning softly.

"The devil with the count and his emeralds! What of Grandmama?" cried Sheppington. "She is bleeding!"

"I will also require a bed or chaise in a quiet room for Her Grace," I continued, ignoring Sheppington's outburst.

Carolus hurried from the room. I heard him shouting instructions in another tongue. Stanislaw and another footman entered the room, gathered up the count, and carried off the portly figure as easily as a young lady holds her fan.

"Be still, Your Grace," I said, setting down the lamp beside the dowager duchess and bending to examine the wound on her scalp. "Your Lordship, please allow me room to work."

After a moment, he sat back.

I took her hand in mine, although I knew what I would see. The empty fingers of her glove depended from her wrist and quivered as I lifted her hand to the light; she had, at some point before she was injured, unbuttoned her glove at the wrist and drawn her hand out through the opening. The better to admire the emeralds? Yet she had not had time to fold away the surplus kidskin. I finished my examination of her hand and gently encircled her wrist with my fingers. Her pulse remained strong. As I probed the wound on her temple, she winced and drew in a sharp breath.

"You may have a head-ache for a few days, but the injury is superficial," I said, the tightness in my chest easing. I gave her a reassuring smile. "Is it possible for you to sit up?"

She breathed deeply, then nodded. "Of course."

With the assistance of Sheppington, she sat up by degrees.

"Do you remember what happened?" I asked.

Holmes paused in his examination of the jewel case and glanced in our direction.

She frowned. "As we entered the room, my attention was upon the glass case. I stepped to the table . . ." She hesitated for only a moment, a faint glow touching her cheeks. "I did not notice anything amiss before the lights were extinguished. And then . . ." Her brows drew together. "I . . . I do not remember anything more."

A soft cough announced Carolus's return.

"I have prepared a room for Her Grace," he said. "And sent a messenger for the *policja*."

"If you cannot stand," I said, "the footmen can carry you—"

She lifted her chin. "Hilary will assist me."

"Certainly, Grandmama." The viscount leaned over, his arm encircling her shoulders.

I lent my strength on her other side. At one point she bowed her head as if overcome. Holmes uttered a brief exclamation and swooped in, but his concern was unnecessary. She gained her feet without experiencing any further weakness.

Despite Holmes's obvious impatience, I insisted she pause a moment before proceeding. Once assured that she would not succumb, I allowed her, supported by her grandson, to leave the room.

From outside, I heard Denbeigh cry "Mother!" before Holmes drew me toward the broken window. Cold air poured into the room. I took a deep breath.

"Quickly, Watson! The police will arrive any moment. I am certain you observed several deep scorings raked across the count's face, as if from fingernails. Is it possible that she inflicted such wounds?"

The question did not surprise me. Naturally, Holmes would have noticed my reaction to the evidence on her fingers and wish to ascertain the cause. That did not mean I welcomed his enquiry, however.

I sighed. "Yes."

"As I suspected." Holmes sounded extremely satisfied.

"Her actions must have been defensive!" Any other option was simply unthinkable. "Surely the count attacked her . . ."

"Do you truly believe a lady of her years was capable of repelling his determined attack?" His voice was hard as flint. "And what of the emeralds?"

I looked from the empty jewel case to the broken window.

"No. No, it cannot be, Holmes. She cannot be responsible."

"You are thinking with your heart and not your mind, Watson! Does not the evidence point to Her Grace surprising the count with a blow of sufficient force to stagger him?"

"With what?" I gestured to the room. "There is nothing she could use as a weapon."

Holmes pointed to a brass poker lying in a shadowed corner. I had not noticed it before.

"There is blood upon the end," he said.

How could this be? In her right mind, the dowager duchess would never be capable of such actions. Was Denbeigh correct to be concerned that his mother suffered from kleptomania? If so, could her disease have progressed to a violent manifestation with such rapidity?

Holmes continued. "After she removed the jewels from their case, the count must have recovered enough to lunge at her. She fended off his attack, in the course of which he fell and struck his head. Either she was already in the process of ridding herself of the jewels before this occurred and lost consciousness immediately, or she was able to break the window and toss the jewels outside before succumbing to her injury."

"If what you say is true, Holmes, and I must admit that I fervently hope you are wrong, it must be a direct result of this insidious disease. She is most certainly not at fault, and it might be possible to salvage her reputation." I turned toward the door. "Let us retrieve the emeralds before the police arrive."

"Too late, I fear," replied Holmes as voices rose in the receiving room. "However, we do have one further clue as to what occurred." He thrust his hand into his coat pocket and withdrew it far enough for me to catch a glimpse of glittering emerald and fiery diamond against his palm.

I started at the unexpected sight. "Good gracious! But where …"

He returned the gem to his pocket and smoothed back his hair.

"The least of the jewels," he said softly. "It lay beneath her, and I was able to retrieve it without her knowledge."

Misery kept me mute.

A hoarse cough from the door caught our attention. A large constable stood on the threshold, holding his hat and frowning.

"Now, wot's all this then?"

* * * *

I excused myself and left Holmes to explain the situation to the constable, for I still had my patient to attend. Her Grace rested in a cheerful morning room, while Sheppington sat on a footstool by her side. With a thunderous expression, Denbeigh paced the length of the room.

There was little I could do save admonish Denbeigh for worrying his mother, assure myself that her pulse remained strong, and vow to return again in a quarter hour to ensure she continued to improve.

I closed the morning room door behind me and turned to face a tremendous bustle and clamour. Apparently the police had arrived in force while I attended the dowager duchess, for a handful of constables were endeavoring to contain the count's guests in the ballroom. I returned to the receiving room.

"There you are, Watson," said Holmes. "You remember Mr Athelney Jones of Scotland Yard."

He indicated a stout, ruddy-faced man, whose small, bright eyes nearly disappeared into heavy folds of flesh.

"Of course I do," I replied, as Jones wheezed a greeting.

"Bad business, this," said Jones. "Dowager Duchess of Penfield attacked, eh? Not to mention that foreign count. I've examined the room and will need to ask them a few questions, of course."

"Her Grace is still quite shaken and should not be disturbed," I said firmly. Certainly too shaken to be questioned by Jones. "I believe Count von Kratzov's physician is attending him now. He will be able to answer as to the count's current condition. When I last saw the count, he was unconscious."

"Ah." Jones pursed his lips. "You were there when the attack occurred?"

"Not in the room, no." I explained what I had seen. "I cannot tell you more."

"Just so, Doctor." Jones nodded vigorously, his jowls quivering like the dewlaps of a dog on the scent. "Mr Holmes showed me the smashed case. No sign of the jewels. What were they? Diamonds?"

"The von Kratzov emeralds are priceless and renowned throughout Europe," replied Holmes.

"Are they, indeed?" Jones did not appear impressed.

"That is why the count instituted so many precautions: the locked door, the trusted servant stationed outside, the jewels themselves housed in a case," I added.

"Which did nothing to prevent the theft," Jones said bluntly. "So although the window was broken, the iron bars are too closely spaced to allow even a child to enter or exit. Common sense tells us the glass was broken by accident." He tugged at the waistcoat of his grey suit. "The facts are clear, gentlemen. The thief slipped by the count's man and entered the room. He then pocketed the emeralds, but before he could leave, the count and Her Grace surprised him. The thief attacked them, and after you and Mr Holmes here entered, he escaped in the confusion."

"A most interesting theory," said Holmes. I met his gaze, but did not speak.

"Facts, Mr Holmes! Facts! As I've had occasion to remind you before, you should avoid theories and focus strictly on the facts. There can be no other explanation that fits the facts you and the doctor have presented."

As he spoke, a constable approached and waited to one side. Jones lifted a finger and directed his attention to the young man. Frowning at Holmes and me, the constable murmured to Jones.

"Good, good!" said Jones, then turned to us. "Excuse me, gentlemen."

Holmes waited until Jones and the constable hurried off in the direction of the ballroom.

"Now is our opportunity, Watson. Let us see what is outside the broken window." He caught up a lamp and hurried toward a baize-covered door.

Fortunately, we were unobserved as we entered the servants's hall. I glanced about the dimly lit corridor with dun-coloured walls and cocoa-nut matting on the floor—a stark contrast to the richly appointed apartments that lay on the opposite side of the door. The air smelt faintly of cabbage and beer.

"Do you truly believe we will find the jewels?" I asked, following him closely.

"I most certainly do not believe in Mr Athelney Jones's theory of a thief who, through no doubt supernatural means, entered the room, stole the emeralds, attacked Her Grace and the count, and then disappeared into the *ewigkeit*." Holmes paused as a young woman with a doubtful expression, carrying an armful of linens, hurried past.

After several turns and one brief detour, we gained entry to the cobbled yard. Several grooms bustled about purposefully, while a few others leaned against the wall, smoking their pipes. I gasped as the cold struck me like a blow and wished I had collected my coat and hat first.

"This way," Holmes said, as always indifferent to the temperature.

I hurried to follow his long strides as he crossed the yard and turned onto Chapel Street. After a glance at the façade to locate the broken window, he handed me the lamp. A locked iron gate guarded the stair that gave access to the deep channel between house and pavement. Holmes nimbly leapt over the gate and made his way down the stair.

I raised the lamp, illuminating the narrow well. Holmes dropped to his knees, heedless of the decaying leaf mould and spots of damp on the pavement.

"Where are they?" he muttered as he ran his hands through the debris. "They *must* be here. Watson, examine the street and the kerb."

I did as he bade, but saw nothing save the usual effluvia.

"There is no trace of the jewels here. Unless they were discovered by a passerby and taken away."

"Or retrieved by an accomplice," he replied. "Which would belie the diagnosis of kleptomania."

"You have gone too far, Holmes. I refuse to countenance such nonsense! Why, she could no more plan and execute such a devious and audacious theft than I could!"

"I fear you underestimate your capabilities, my dear fellow, as well as those of Her Grace." He climbed the stair and vaulted the rail again. "However, the fact of the matter is the emeralds are not here."

"I must admit that I am relieved." I cast a despairing eye over his stained knees and filthy hands. Holmes followed my gaze.

He raised one brow and withdrew his handkerchief, wiping his hands. I sighed. Mrs Hudson would have something to say when she discovered the damage to his evening clothes.

"I have gone wrong, Watson. Very wrong."

Holmes thrust his grimy handkerchief into his pocket, and we returned to the house in silence.

Slowly we retraced our steps through the corridors. As we turned a corner, Holmes suddenly cried out and fell to his knees.

"Light, Watson!"

I held the lamp near. Nose almost to the floorboards, Holmes extended a finger and delicately brushed a small spot of white powder at the edge of the cocoa-nut matting. It glinted in the light.

"Holmes, is that glass?"

"Yes, Watson!" He raised his face, eyes shining with excitement. "I have been a fool, and you may remind me of the fact whenever I become enamoured of my own genius. In this matter we are now in complete agreement: the Dowager Duchess of Penfield is innocent of this crime."

"You are truly convinced of her innocence because of a dusting of powdered glass?" I cried. "But how?"

"Through the application of logic, my dear fellow." Rising, Holmes snatched the lamp from my hands and scrutinized the corridor. "Ah!"

Lamp held high, he strode down the hall until he reached a corner. Bending low, he examined another small spot on the matting.

"More glass?" I asked, frowning. "How can this be significant?"

He glanced up at me. "Where have we recently encountered a quantity of such glass?"

"In the drawing room where the emeralds were displayed."

"This pulverised glass is the very same glass used in the jewels's display case."

"Can you be certain it is that particular glass? Perhaps a servant broke a goblet or bottle, and a shard was crushed underfoot."

"You may remember the monograph I wrote on the chemical composition of varieties of glass as evidenced through the spectrum, Watson. This is not crystal, nor common pressed glass, nor is it the glass generally used for window-panes. It displays the identical colour signature as the crushed remains of the case."

We followed the faint traces of powdered glass through the house. His gaze fixed upon the floor, Holmes cast about with the lamp, as if he were a modern-day Diogenes. Passing servants looked upon us with confusion, but none dared interrupt.

"What have you found?" I asked as he bent over at the back of an odd little alcove.

He straightened, his keen eyes glinting in the lamplight, and raised his arm. A length of heavy, dark fabric cascaded from his hand.

"It is a cloak," he replied, folding it over his arm. "With a hood."

"Perhaps a servant dropped it," I said, although my assertion sounded feeble even to my ears.

"Perhaps. But does its presence here not suggest another possibility?"

I frowned. "Not to me. The cloak cannot be germane to the problem at hand, for this niche does not lead anywhere. Look about you; there are no doors or windows, nor even a cupboard where the thief could hide."

Holmes turned and started back the way we had come. "Watson, recall the words of our colleague, Mr Athelney Jones. We must deal with facts."

I trailed behind him. "Even if those facts are meaningless as a whole?"

"Ah, but are they truly meaningless?" He glanced back at me over his shoulder. "Come, Watson. You know my methods; use them. There is only one way to assemble these facts into a meaningful pattern."

He stopped before the baize door leading to the receiving room and set down the lamp. I folded my arms. "What does the evidence reveal to you?"

"Why, everything," Holmes replied lightly, as he opened the door.

"Everything? Including the name of the thief?"

"Everything, Watson. Including the names of the thieves." He walked into the receiving room, the door swinging closed behind him.

"Wait, Holmes!" I dashed through the door. "Thieves?"

Much to my aggravation, Holmes refused to say more. Instead of answering my questions, he sent a young constable for Mr Athelney Jones.

Before Jones arrived, I heard a quiet cough at my shoulder and turned.

Carolus bowed. "I beg your pardon, Doctor."

"Yes?"

"Her Grace requests your presence."

"Certainly."

I excused myself and followed Carolus to the chamber where the dowager duchess rested. Sheppington still sat by her side.

"At last!" he cried, leaping to his feet.

Denbeigh ceased pacing and looked at me expectantly.

"My mother wishes—" began Denbeigh, breaking off when Her Grace raised her hand.

"Thank you for responding so promptly, Doctor," she said. "Has Mr Holmes any solution to the mysterious events surrounding the theft of the emeralds that will clear me of suspicion?"

I sat beside her in the chair vacated by the viscount.

"You understand I cannot speak for Holmes," I said. "Rest assured, however, that his investigations will soon be concluded, and they are leading in an entirely different direction."

"I should hope so!" Denbeigh said, posture rigid.

"I am glad to hear it." She sighed, and for an instant I glimpsed the deeply troubled woman beneath the public persona. The moment passed quickly as she exerted her iron will and continued: "I am certain that I have recovered sufficiently to return home, yet agree with Maurice and Hilary that it would be prudent to request your opinion before venturing forth."

"Very sensible," I replied. My examination was of necessity superficial, and when I had finished, I released her wrist with a smile. "You are a remarkable woman."

She laughed. "You forgot to add 'for my age,' Doctor."

"For a woman of any age," I asserted and helped her to rise.

Although her step was firm and her carriage erect, she leaned heavily upon me as we slowly walked down the corridor, followed closely by Denbeigh and Sheppington.

We gained the receiving room, where Holmes, no longer carrying the cloak, stood deep in conference with Jones. Carolus listened at a respectful distance.

"A moment, Doctor," she said, releasing my arm. "Mr Holmes, I believe you have made progress in your investigation?"

"I have indeed," said Holmes. "If you will permit me to detain you for a few minutes, I would like to demonstrate how the attack upon you and the count, as well as the theft of the emeralds, occurred."

I glared at Holmes and turned to my patient. "Your Grace, I believe this is most unwise!"

My exclamation was lost amidst the chorus of voices evincing surprise and disbelief at Holmes's request, which continued until Her Grace nodded once.

"Very well, Mr Holmes." She quelled Denbeigh's vehement objections with a glance.

Jones entered the drawing room first, while a constable remained stationed by the door. Holmes quickly ushered in Her Grace, Denbeigh, and Sheppington, followed by Carolus. When Jones questioned the latter's appearance, Holmes raised his hand.

"In the absence of Count von Kratzov," Holmes said, "I have requested that his private secretary attend us, so that he may correct any errors I might make regarding the details of the display."

"Get on with it, Mr Holmes," Jones grumbled.

I have always maintained that Holmes, despite his protestations to the contrary, is a consummate showman. To set the stage, he lowered the light until the room was cloaked in shadows. Then he positioned Her Grace in the centre of the room by the overturned table and asked Carolus to take the count's place opposite her.

"Play-acting!" muttered Jones, but he did not object further.

"Upon your entry into the room, your attention was immediately caught by the sight of those magnificent emeralds," Holmes said, addressing Her Grace. "As you admired them, the count stood by your side. His remarks became more personal and intrusive. When he pressed close, becoming increasingly familiar, you struck out at him and withdrew to the window."

The colour drained from her face, and I hurried to her side. She waved me away.

"Continue," she said, her voice firm.

Holmes lifted one brow. "Before he could pursue you, the lights were extinguished and there was a sudden commotion: the sounds of a struggle and breaking glass, the grunts of the combatants. In the faint illumination from the window, you watched as indistinct shapes wreaked havoc in the room."

Her hand crept to her throat and she nodded, her eyes dark with the memory.

"I recall it all now," she whispered. "A man stumbled toward me. It was the count, his face streaming with blood, his hands reaching . . ." She shuddered. "He struck me on the temple, a blow that sent me reeling. I fended him off, and he moved away with a cry, but my head swam and I staggered, grasping at the curtains for support." She looked at Holmes, her brows drawn together in bewilderment. "I do not remember more."

"That is hardly surprising," I said, stepping to her side. "Holmes, I really—"

"No, Doctor," she interrupted. Her voice trembled. "I must know what happened. Mr Holmes, can you tell me who attacked the count, and how did he enter and leave a locked room?"

"Certainly, Your Grace." By some trick of the light, Holmes's eyes shone like a cat's. "I shall answer the latter first." He strode to the far wall and ran his long fingers across the moulding.

"Mr Holmes," began Jones. "What are you—?"

His question died upon his lips as, with a soft creak, a portion of the wall swung open. A secret panel! I was scarcely able to believe my eyes. Beyond the opening, I could make out the small niche that Holmes and I had explored earlier.

"Good God!" cried Denbeigh. Sheppington bit back a ripe oath.

"Capital, Holmes! A palpable fact!" Jones smiled and tugged on the lapels of his coat. "I asked for facts, and you have provided me with a corker!"

"Mr Holmes, you have exceeded my expectations," Her Grace said, sounding a trifle breathless. "How did you ever discover this?"

Holmes explained his discovery of the crushed glass. "The traces we found were of the same variety used in the jewels's display case, and the trail led to an alcove in the servants's hall that is visible through the door."

"In addition," he continued, "the thief did not retrace his steps, as the single set of tracks clearly showed. Therefore, it was clear that the thief entered the servants's hall at that location, directly from this chamber."

"So the thief must still have traces of glass in his boots," I said.

"Exactly, Watson." Holmes pointed to the area of powdered glass on the floor beside the hearth. "The thief trod in the glass there, and when he exited, he left a trail—Constable! Stop that man!" Holmes cried.

Denbeigh started.

Confused, I glanced about the chamber.

Carolus struggled in the grasp of the burly constable, shouting what sounded like pleas in a foreign language, his face pale with terror. He must have surreptitiously edged toward the door as Holmes outlined the evidence.

"If you examine the soles of his shoes," Holmes said to Jones, "you will discover traces of glass embedded in the leather—the same glass as that of the smashed jewel case."

"And the emeralds," Jones said triumphantly. "He must have taken them after he attacked his master."

Carolus ceased his struggles and turned to Holmes. "Mr Holmes, you must believe me! I never meant to harm anyone. When my master and Her Grace entered, I hid in the shadows, but I could not stand by and watch the count molest her."

She shuddered once, then breathed deeply, lifting her chin. I could not but admire her strength.

"Why are you listening to this blackguard, Mr Holmes!" Sheppington pushed his way past his uncle and glared at Carolus. "He has deceived us all."

"I very much doubt that he is the only person in this room who is not speaking the truth," replied Holmes with a cold look at the young man. He addressed Carolus again. "But what of the emeralds?"

"I do not have them!" he asserted.

"Then who does?" Holmes asked, his voice implacable.

"I do not know his name, and I never saw his face." Carolus bowed his head. "He came to me, and threatened to reveal . . ." His throat worked as he swallowed.

"It is not uncommon for opium addicts to be blackmailed," said Holmes.

Carolus stared at him. "How did you—?"

Holmes waved negligently. "The characteristic sallow complexion, the wide pupil, a trace of the distinct odour . . . Your vice was obvious to me the moment we met."

"I see," Carolus whispered. "He knew of the secret panel. He instructed me to ensure that the emeralds were displayed in this room and to steal them tonight. After doing so, I was to leave them wrapped in a handkerchief behind a vase in the receiving room. When I checked after arranging for the count to be carried to his chambers, they were not there. I know nothing more!"

"All this sounds extremely dubious to me," Jones grunted. "Mr Holmes, do you believe this ruffian?"

"I do indeed." Holmes surveyed the room. He reached into his pocket and then lifted his clenched fist. All eyes were upon him. He opened his hand, revealing the emerald he had discovered beneath Her Grace.

"You may wish to check the jewels you received, Your Lordship, for I believe you are missing one."

As he spoke, Denbeigh drew himself up and fixed his cold gaze upon Holmes.

"How *dare* you imply—"

"I recognize that voice!" cried Carolus, pointing at Denbeigh. "It is he!"

"The villain lies to save himself," Denbeigh said, turning to the door. "I will not stand here and—"

"No," Her Grace whispered, sagging against me.

"Grandmama!" Sheppington rushed up and supported her other arm, but she had already mastered her momentary weakness.

"Maurice." Her steely tones cut him off abruptly. "Show us the contents of your pockets."

Complexion the colour of parchment, Denbeigh turned from face to stern face. A constable approached.

"Do not lay hands upon me!" He gazed imploringly at the dowager duchess. "Mother, you cannot—"

"Show us, Maurice."

"There is no escape, Your Lordship," Holmes said and held out his hand.

With a sigh, Denbeigh reached into his coat pocket, then deposited a small parcel wrapped in a handkerchief into Holmes's waiting hand. Holmes quickly untied the knots and opened the linen. The gems inside glittered with cold fire.

Jones shook himself as if roused from a deep slumber and took charge of the situation. A phalanx of constables removed Denbeigh and Carolus from the chamber, while Her Grace sent instructions to the family solicitor.

"I shall also ensure Carolus is represented well," she said, Sheppington standing at her side. "For I feel a certain amount of responsibility for this situation." She dismissed my protestations with a sad shake of her head.

"Your Grace, I am certain you have many questions," Holmes began.

"Thank you, Mr Holmes, but I am a trifle fatigued." She gave him a weary smile. "Hilary and I shall call upon you and Dr Watson on the morrow. You may answer my questions then. For now, I would like Hilary to take me home."

The following morning, Holmes and I perused the newspapers over breakfast, and I was relieved there was no mention of the incident.

"It will do nothing to prevent rumours from flying about," said Holmes in response to my observation. "Fortunately, this sort of occurrence is handled with discretion and seldom goes to trial."

True to her word, Her Grace, accompanied by Sheppington, called upon us a little later. As she entered our chamber, I was pleased to see that her step was as firm, her carriage as elegant as usual. When she lifted her heavy veil, however, traces of the emotional and physical toll of the previous evening were writ clearly upon her features, for she had apparently eschewed the use of cosmetics and artifice to hide her injuries.

"You are well?" I asked.

"Thanks to your assistance and care," she replied. Settling upon the sofa, her grandson beside her, she declined our offer of refreshment with a weary air.

"There is still much to be arranged," she confessed in quiet, dignified tones. "My son's perfidy extends further than I had suspected."

"Yet you did suspect something amiss," said Holmes. He leaned against the hearth, regarding her gravely. "You instructed Viscount Sheppington to monitor His Lordship's activities. He was unable, or possibly unwilling, to disguise himself as effectively as Lord Maurice, and thereby gained a reputation as a connoisseur of certain unsavoury practices."

The young man's countenance darkened. "When I began, I did not realise I would be haunting venues where a disguise would be essential, Mr Holmes. That fact was quickly brought home to me, but by that point, I was already tarred by vice's brush." He shrugged. "I can only hope that the rumour-mongers will soon discover another object of interest and I can endeavour to restore my character."

Her Grace took his hand and pressed it gently. "I never meant for you to suffer so, dear boy."

"Do not vex yourself, Your Lordship," said Holmes. "The most cursory glance at the newspapers will supply a variety of individuals with reputations far more scandalous than yours. Besides, isn't it often considered desirable for a young scion of the nobility to have a faintly dubious past, above which he can rise?"

"I say!" cried Sheppington.

Her Grace assayed a faint smile, yet her lips trembled. "We can only hope that is indeed the case, Mr Holmes."

I rose from my chair. "But why? Why did His Lordship court exposure and disgrace?"

"For the money," said Sheppington. "Although his vices were few, they were costly. Gambling at cards and on the horses, and his mistress alone . . ." He glanced at his grandmother, his cheeks colouring.

Holmes nodded. "When His Lordship encountered Carolus smoking opium in a den of depravity, he conceived of the plan to steal the emeralds. He was familiar with the count's house and its hidden doorway, for it had been in your family for many years, had it not?"

"We resided there for several years while he was a child," she said. "Even then, Maurice was always poking into corners and winkling out everyone's secrets."

"Through his unsavoury associates," continued Holmes, "His Lordship knew he could dispose of the gems, or alternatively, he could hold them for ransom. Either way, he would benefit."

"Unfortunately for Carolus, he became my son's dupe," said Her Grace. "And yet I cannot help but be grateful to him, for he defended me from the count's advances at some considerable risk to himself."

"Addicts are not necessarily criminals or depraved individuals," I said, not looking at Holmes. "Indeed, there are several private clinics that have successfully weaned these unfortunate individuals from the sources of their addiction. If Your Grace would consider arranging for his treatment at one such facility, it would certainly repay his actions on your behalf."

"An excellent suggestion, Doctor." She nodded. "If I may, I shall ask for a few recommendations."

"Of course." I bowed.

"Now I must broach a more delicate matter, one I wish to conduct without intermediaries." She stood, opened her reticule, and withdrew an envelope. "Mr Holmes, your assistance in this matter has been invaluable to me and to all of my family, even the one exposed by your investigations. I hope you will accept the enclosed as a token of my gratitude for your efforts."

"I was honoured to be of service." Holmes accepted the envelope, setting it to one side.

"And you, Doctor," she said, turning to me with a smile. "How can I ever find the words to thank you?"

Momentarily speechless at the warmth of her regard, I bowed again. "It was entirely my pleasure."

"I know you would not accept any gift of great value, but I hope you will permit me to present you with this small keepsake." She pressed a small, gold locket into my hand.

"Your Grace!" I said, opening the locket. Inside rested an exquisite miniature portrait of the dowager duchess, obviously painted at the time I first met her. "I am honoured and will keep it always."

"And now, gentlemen, if you will excuse us," she said. "I have an appointment with my solicitor. Hilary, will you see to the carriage?"

"Of course, Grandmother. Thank you, Mr Holmes, Doctor." He hurried out the door.

Holmes gravely bowed over her hand, and she allowed me the pleasure of seeing her to the door. Her carriage waited at the kerb. With a wistful smile, she pressed my hand before turning and crossing the pavement. Sheppington handed her into the brougham, then joined her.

I returned to our apartments, unaccountably melancholy. Had not Holmes solved the case to Her Grace's satisfaction? Taking my seat beside the fire, I picked up a medical journal but did not open it.

"She is a woman of immense strength, Watson." Holmes sounded almost kind. "I am certain she will weather any storm of gossip or public exposure regarding her son's behaviour with her usual dignity."

I sighed. "You are right, of course. I wish there were some way for me to assist her through this horrible period. If there were not more than thirty years separating our ages . . ."

A quiet knock on the door interrupted me.

"Come," said Holmes.

Mrs Hudson entered, a small crease between her brows. "A messenger brought this at the behest of Viscount Sheppington." She held out her hand. In her palm rested a small gold cigarette case.

"Good Lord, Holmes." I glanced at the table where I had last seen it resting. "Isn't that the case from—" I stopped, remembering in time the gentleman's request for anonymity.

Holmes laughed. "It is indeed, my dear fellow." He took the case from Mrs Hudson. "Was there a message?"

"Only that he would endeavour to be vigilant, but that it might be necessary to call upon you in future." She shook her head. "I hope you understand it, Mr Holmes."

"Thank you, Mrs Hudson."

I gazed in consternation at my friend, for it was impossible for me to conceal my disappointment at this evidence of Her Grace's continuing kleptomania.

He waited until she departed before continuing. "Take heart, Watson. It is a small flaw in an otherwise sterling character, and yet I suspect we have not seen the last of Her Grace, the Dowager Duchess of Penfield." He glanced out the window. "Since the afternoon has turned fine, I suggest we take a turn about the park."

"Excellent idea, Holmes." As I collected my coat and hat, I glanced at the locket depending from my watch chain and smiled.

✗

Note: Carla Coupe's story was *very* loosely based on the radioplay "The Adventure of the Elusive Emerald," by Anthony Boucher and Denis Greene, originally broadcast on December 21, 1946.

COMING NEXT TIME . . .

Sherlock Holmes Mystery Magazine #5 will be a special Sherlockian Fiction issue, with great new Holmes & Watson stories galore! Not to mention the usual features, poems, cartoons, and more. And, with our successful completion of four "test" issues, we will begin a regular quarterly publication schedule under the watchful helm of editor Marvin Kaye.

Not a subscriber yet? Send $39.95 for the next 4 issues (postage paid) to:

> Wildside Press LLC
> Subscription Dept.
> 9710 Traville Gateway Dr. #234
> Rockville MD 20850

You can also subscribe online at www.wildsidebooks.com.

THE ADVENTURE OF THE RESIDENT PATIENT

by Arthur Conan Doyle

Glancing over the somewhat incoherent series of Memoirs with which I have endeavoured to illustrate a few of the mental peculiarities of my friend Mr. Sherlock Holmes, I have been struck by the difficulty which I have experienced in picking out examples which shall in every way answer my purpose. For in those cases in which Holmes has performed some tour de force of analytical reasoning, and has demonstrated the value of his peculiar methods of investigation, the facts themselves have often been so slight or so commonplace that I could not feel justified in laying them before the public. On the other hand, it has frequently happened that he has been concerned in some research where the facts have been of the most remarkable and dramatic character, but where the share which he has himself taken in determining their causes has been less pronounced than I, as his biographer, could wish. The small matter which I have chronicled under the heading of "A Study in Scarlet," and that other later one connected with the loss of the Gloria Scott, may serve as examples of this Scylla and Charybdis which are forever threatening the historian. It may be that in the business of which I am now about to write the part which my friend played is not sufficiently accentuated; and yet the whole train of circumstances is so remarkable that I cannot bring myself to omit it entirely from this series.

I cannot be sure of the exact date, for some of my memoranda upon the matter have been mislaid, but it must have been towards the end of the first year during which Holmes and I shared chambers in Baker Street. It was boisterous October weather, and we had both remained indoors all day, I because I feared with my shaken health to face the keen autumn wind, while he was deep in some of those abstruse chemical investigations which absorbed him utterly as long as he was engaged upon them. Towards evening, however, the breaking of a test-tube brought his research to a premature ending, and he sprang up from his chair with an exclamation of impatience and a clouded brow.

"A day's work ruined, Watson," said he, striding across to the window. "Ha! The stars are out and the wind has fallen. What do you say to a ramble through London?"

I was weary of our little sitting-room and gladly acquiesced. For three hours we strolled about together, watching the ever-changing kaleidoscope of life as it ebbs and flows through Fleet Street and the Strand. His characteristic talk, with its keen observance of detail and subtle power of inference held me amused and enthralled. It was ten o'clock before we reached Baker Street again. A brougham was waiting at our door.

"Hum! A doctor's — general practitioner, I perceive," said Holmes. "Not been long in practice, but has had a good deal to do. Come to consult us, I fancy! Lucky we came back!"

I was sufficiently conversant with Holmes's methods to be able to follow his reasoning, and to see that the nature and state of the various medical instruments in the wicker basket which hung in the lamplight inside the brougham had given him the data for his swift deduction. The light in our window above showed that this late visit was indeed intended for us. With some curiosity as to what could have sent a brother medico to us at such an hour, I followed Holmes into our sanctum.

A pale, taper-faced man with sandy whiskers rose up from a chair by the fire as we entered. His age may not have been more than three or four and thirty, but his haggard expression and unhealthy hue told of a life which has sapped his strength and robbed him of his youth. His manner was nervous and shy, like that of a sensitive gentleman, and the thin white hand which he laid on the mantelpiece as he rose was that of an artist rather than of a surgeon. His dress was quiet and sombre — a black frock-coat, dark trousers, and a touch of colour about his necktie.

"Good-evening, doctor," said Holmes, cheerily. "I am glad to see that you have only been waiting a very few minutes."

"You spoke to my coachman, then?"

"No, it was the candle on the side-table that told me. Pray resume your seat and let me know how I can serve you."

"My name is Doctor Percy Trevelyan," said our visitor, "and I live at 403 Brook Street."

"Are you not the author of a monograph upon obscure nervous lesions?" I asked.

His pale cheeks flushed with pleasure at hearing that his work was known to me.

"I so seldom hear of the work that I thought it was quite dead," said he. "My publishers gave me a most discouraging account of its sale. You are yourself, I presume, a medical man?"

"A retired army surgeon."

"My own hobby has always been nervous disease. I should wish to make it an absolute speciality, but, of course, a man must take what he can get at first. This, however, is beside the question, Mr. Sherlock Holmes, and I quite appreciate how valuable your time is. The fact is that a very singular train of events has occurred recently at my house in Brook Street, and to-night they came to such a head that I felt it was quite impossible for me to wait another hour before asking for your advice and assistance."

Sherlock Holmes sat down and lit his pipe. "You are very welcome to both," said he. "Pray let me have a detailed account of what the circumstances are which have disturbed you."

"One or two of them are so trivial," said Dr. Trevelyan, "that really I am almost ashamed to mention them. But the matter is so inexplicable, and the recent turn which it has taken is so elaborate, that I shall lay it all before you, and you shall judge what is essential and what is not.

"I am compelled, to begin with, to say something of my own college career. I am a London University man, you know, and I am sure that your will not think that I am unduly singing my own praises if I say that my student career was considered by my professors to be a very promising one. After I had graduated I continued to devote myself to research, occupying a minor position in King's College Hospital, and I was fortunate enough to excite considerable interest by my research into the pathology of catalepsy, and finally to win the Bruce Pinkerton prize and medal by the monograph on nervous lesions to which your friend has just alluded. I should not go too far if I were to say that there was a general impression at that time that a distinguished career lay before me.

"But the one great stumbling-block lay in my want of capital. As you will readily understand, a specialist who aims high is compelled to start in one of a dozen streets in the Cavendish Square quarter, all of which entail enormous rents and furnishing expenses. Besides this preliminary outlay, he must be prepared to keep himself for some years, and to hire a presentable carriage and horse. To do this was quite beyond my power, and I could only hope that by economy I might in ten years' time save enough to enable me to put up my plate. Suddenly, however, an unexpected incident opened up quite a new prospect to me.

"This was a visit from a gentleman of the name of Blessington, who was a complete stranger to me. He came up to my room one morning, and plunged into business in an instant.

"'You are the same Percy Trevelyan who has had so distinguished a career and won a great prize lately?' said he.

"I bowed.

"'Answer me frankly,' he continued, 'for you will find it to your interest to do so. You have all the cleverness which makes a successful man. Have you the tact?'

"I could not help smiling at the abruptness of the question.

"'I trust that I have my share,' I said.

"'Any bad habits? Not drawn towards drink, eh?'

"'Really, sir!' I cried.

"'Quite right! That's all right! But I was bound to ask. With all these qualities, why are you not in practice?'

"I shrugged my shoulders.

"'Come, come!' said he, in his bustling way. 'It's the old story. More in your brains than in your pocket, eh? What would you say if I were to start you in Brook Street?'

"I stared at him in astonishment.

"'Oh, it's for my sake, not for yours,' he cried. 'I'll be perfectly frank with you, and if it suits you it will suit me very well. I have a few thousands to invest, d'ye see, and I think I'll sink them in you.'

"'But why?' I gasped.

"'Well, it's just like any other speculation, and safer than most.'

"'What am I to do, then?'

"'I'll tell you. I'll take the house, furnish it, pay the maids, and run the whole place. All you have to do is just to wear out your chair in the consulting-room. I'll let you have pocket-money and everything. Then you hand over to me three quarters of what you earn, and you keep the other quarter for yourself.'

"This was the strange proposal, Mr. Holmes, with which the man Blessington approached me. I won't weary you with the account of how we bargained and negotiated. It ended in my moving into the house next Lady-day, and starting in practice on very much the same conditions as he had suggested. He came himself to live with me in the character of a resident patient. His heart was weak, it appears, and he needed constant medical supervision. He turned the two best rooms of the first floor into a sitting-room and bedroom for himself. He was a man of singular habits, shunning company and very seldom going out. His life was irregular, but in one respect he was regularity itself. Every evening, at the same hour, he walked into the consulting-room, examined the books, put down five and three-pence for every guinea that I had earned, and carried the rest off to the strong-box in his own room.

"I may say with confidence that he never had occasion to regret his speculation. From the first it was a success. A few good cases and the reputation which I had won in the hospital brought me rapidly to the front, and during the last few years I have made him a rich man.

"So much, Mr. Holmes, for my past history and my relations with Mr. Blessington. It only remains for me now to tell you what has occurred to bring me here to-night.

"Some weeks ago Mr. Blessington came down to me in, as it seemed to me, a state of considerable agitation. He spoke of some burglary which, he said, had been committed in the West End, and he appeared, I remember, to be quite unnecessarily excited about it, declaring that a day should not pass before we should add stronger bolts to our windows and doors. For a week he continued to be in a peculiar state of restlessness, peering continually out of the windows, and ceasing to take the short walk which had usually been the prelude to his dinner. From his manner it struck me that he was in mortal dread of something or somebody, but when I questioned him upon the point he became so offensive that I was compelled to drop the subject. Gradually, as time passed, his fears appeared to die away, and he had renewed his former habits, when a fresh event reduced him to the pitiable state of prostration in which he now lies.

"What happened was this. Two days ago I received the letter which I now read to you. Neither address nor date is attached to it.

"'A Russian nobleman who is now resident in England,' it runs, 'would be glad to avail himself of the professional assistance of Dr. Percy Trevelyan. He has been for some years a victim to cataleptic attacks, on which, as is well known, Dr. Trevelyan is an authority. He proposes to call at about quarter past six to-morrow evening, if Dr. Trevelyan will make it convenient to be at home.'

"This letter interested me deeply, because the chief difficulty in the study of catalepsy is the rareness of the disease. You may believe, than, that I was in my consulting-room when, at the appointed hour, the page showed in the patient.

"He was an elderly man, thin, demure, and common-place — by no means the conception one forms of a Russian nobleman. I was much more struck by the appearance of his companion. This was a tall young man, surprisingly handsome, with a dark, fierce face, and the limbs and chest of a Hercules. He had his hand under the other's arm as they entered, and helped him to a chair with a tenderness which one would hardly have expected from his appearance.

"'You will excuse my coming in, doctor,' said he to me, speaking English with a slight lisp. 'This is my father, and his health is a matter of the most overwhelming importance to me.'

"I was touched by this filial anxiety. 'You would, perhaps, care to remain during the consultation?' said I.

"'Not for the world,' he cried with a gesture of horror. 'It is more painful to me than I can express. If I were to see my father in one of these dreadful seizures I am convinced that I should never survive it. My own nervous system is an exceptionally sensitive one. With your permission, I will remain in the waiting-room while you go into my father's case.'

"To this, of course, I assented, and the young man withdrew. The patient and I then plunged into a discussion of his case, of which I took exhaustive notes. He was not remarkable for intelligence, and his answers were frequently obscure, which I attributed to his limited acquaintance with our language. Suddenly, however, as I sat writing, he cased to give any answer at all to my inquiries, and on my turning towards him I was shocked to see that he was sitting bolt upright in his chair, staring at me with a perfectly blank and rigid face. He was again in the grip of his mysterious malady.

"My first feeling, as I have just said, was one of pity and horror. My second, I fear, was rather one of professional satisfaction. I made notes of my patient's pulse and temperature, tested the rigidity of his muscles, and examined his reflexes. There was nothing markedly abnormal in any of these conditions, which harmonised with my former experiences. I had obtained good results in such cases by the inhalation of nitrite of amyl, and the present seemed an admirable opportunity of testing its virtues. The bottle was downstairs in my laboratory, so leaving my patient seated in his chair, I ran down to get it. There was some little delay in finding it — five minutes, let us say — and then I returned. Imagine my amazement to find the room empty and the patient gone.

"Of course, my first act was to run into the waiting-room. The son had gone also. The hall door had been closed, but not shut. My page who admits patients is a new boy and by no means quick. He waits downstairs, and runs up to show patients out when I ring the consulting-room bell. He had heard nothing, and the affair remained a complete mystery. Mr. Blessington came in from his walk shortly afterwards, but I did not say anything to him upon the subject, for, to tell the truth, I have got in the way of late of holding as little communication with him as possible.

"Well, I never thought that I should see anything more of the Russian and his son, so you can imagine my amazement when, at the very same hour this evening, they both came marching into my consulting-room, just as they had done before.

"'I feel that I owe you a great many apologies for my abrupt departure yesterday, doctor,' said my patient.

"'I confess that I was very much surprised at it,' said I.

"'Well, the fact is,' he remarked, 'that when I recover from these attacks my mind is always very clouded as to all that has gone before. I woke up in a strange room, as it seemed to me, and made my way out into the street in a sort of dazed way when you were absent.'

"'And I,' said the son, 'seeing my father pass the door of the waiting-room, naturally thought that the consultation had come to an end. It was not until we had reached home that I began to realise the true state of affairs.'

"'Well,' said I, laughing, 'there is no harm done except that you puzzled me terribly; so if you, sir, would kindly step into the waiting-room I shall be happy to continue our consultation which was brought to so abrupt an ending.'

"'For half an hour or so I discussed that old gentleman's symptoms with him, and then, having prescribed for him, I saw him go off upon the arm of his son.

"I have told you that Mr. Blessington generally chose this hour of the day for his exercise. He came in shortly afterwards and passed upstairs. An instant later I heard him running down, and he burst into my consulting-room like a man who is mad with panic.

"'Who has been in my room?' he cried.

"'No one,' said I.

"'It's a lie! He yelled. 'Come up and look!'

"I passed over the grossness of his language, as he seemed half out of his mind with fear. When I went upstairs with him he pointed to several footprints upon the light carpet.

"'D'you mean to say those are mine?' he cried.

"They were certainly very much larger than any which he could have made, and were evidently quite fresh. It rained hard this afternoon, as you know, and my patients were the only people who called. It must have been the case, then, that the man in the waiting-room had, for some unknown reason, while I was busy with the other, ascended to the room of my resident patient. Nothing has been touched or taken, but there were the footprints to prove that the intrusion was an undoubted fact.

"Mr. Blessington seemed more excited over the matter than I should have thought possible, though of course it was enough to disturb anybody's peace of mind. He actually sat crying in an arm-chair, and I could hardly get him to speak coherently. It was his suggestion that I should come round to you, and of course I at once saw the propriety of it, for certainly the incident is a very singular one, though he appears to completely overtake its importance. If you would only come back with me in my brougham, you would at least be able to soothe him, though I can hardly hope that you will be able to explain this remarkable occurrence."

Sherlock Holmes had listened to this long narrative with an intentness which showed me that his interest was keenly aroused. His face was as impassive as ever, but his lids had drooped more heavily over his eyes, and his smoke had curled up more thickly from his pipe to emphasize each curious episode in the doctor's tale. As our visitor concluded, Holmes sprang up without a word, handed me my hat, picked his own from the table, and followed Dr. Trevelyan to the door. Within a quarter of an hour we had been dropped at the door of the physician's residence in Brook Street, one of those sombre, flat-faced houses which one associates with a West-End practice. A small page admitted us, and we began at once to ascend the broad, well-carpeted stair.

But a singular interruption brought us to a standstill. The light at the top was suddenly whisked out, and from the darkness came a reedy, quivering voice.

"I have a pistol," it cried. "I give you my word that I'll fire if you come any nearer."

"This really grows outrageous, Mr. Blessington," cried Dr. Trevelyan.

"Oh, then it is you, doctor," said the voice, with a great heave of relief. "But those other gentlemen, are they what they pretend to be?"

We were conscious of a long scrutiny out of the darkness.

"Yes, yes, it's all right," said the voice at last. "You can come up, and I am sorry if my precautions have annoyed you."

He relit the stair gas as he spoke, and we saw before us a singular-looking man, whose appearance, as well as his voice, testified to his jangled nerves. He was very fat, but had apparently at some time been much fatter, so that the skin hung about his face in loose pouches, like the cheeks of a blood-hound. He was of a sickly colour, and his thin, sandy hair seemed to bristle up with the intensity of his emotion. In his hand he held a pistol, but he thrust it into his pocket as we advanced.

"Good-evening, Mr. Holmes," said he. "I am sure I am very much obliged to you for coming round. No one ever needed your advice more than I do. I suppose that Dr. Trevelyan has told you of this most unwarrantable intrusion into my rooms."

"Quite so," said Holmes. "Who are these two men Mr. Blessington, and why do they wish to molest you?"

"Well, well," said the resident patient, in a nervous fashion, "of course it is hard to say that. You can hardly expect me to answer that, Mr. Holmes."

"Do you mean that you don't know?"

"Come in here, if you please. Just have the kindness to step in here."

He led the way into his bedroom, which was large and comfortably furnished.

"You see that," said he, pointing to a big black box at the end of his bed. "I have never been a very rich man, Mr. Holmes — never made but one investment in my life, as Dr. Trevelyan would tell you. But I don't believe in bankers. I would never trust a banker, Mr. Holmes. Between ourselves, what little I have is in that box, so you can understand what it means to me when unknown people force themselves into my rooms."

Holmes looked at Blessington in his questioning way and shook his head.

"I cannot possibly advise you if you try to deceive me," said he.

"But I have told you everything."

Holmes turned on his heel with a gesture of disgust. "Goodnight, Dr. Trevelyan," said he.

"And no advice for me?" cried Blessington, in a breaking voice.

"My advice to your, sir, is to speak the truth."

A minute later we were in the street and walking for home. We had crossed Oxford Street and were half way down Harley Street before I could get a word from my companion.

"Sorry to bring you out on such a fool's errand, Watson," he said at last. "It is an interesting case, too, at the bottom of it."

"I can make little of it," I confessed.

"Well, it is quite evident that there are two men — more, perhaps, but at least two — who are determined for some reason to get at this fellow Blessington. I have no doubt in my mind that both on the first and on the second occasion that young man penetrated to Blessington's room, while his confederate, by an ingenious device, kept the doctor from interfering."

"And the catalepsy?"

"A fraudulent imitation, Watson, though I should hardly dare to hint as much to our specialist. It is a very easy complaint to imitate. I have done it myself."

"And then?"

"By the purest chance Blessington was out on each occasion. Their reason for choosing so unusual an hour for a consultation was obviously to insure that there should be no other patient in the waiting-room. It just happened, however, that this hour coincided with Blessington's constitutional, which seems to show that they were not very well acquainted with his daily routine. Of course, if they had been merely after plunder they would at least have made some attempt to search for it. Besides, I can read in a man's eye when it is his own skin that he is frightened for. It is inconceivable that this fellow could have made two such vindictive enemies as these appear to be without knowing of it. I hold it, therefore, to be certain that he does know who these men are, and that for reasons of his own he suppresses it. It is just possible that to-morrow may find him in a more communicative mood."

"Is there not one alternative," I suggested, "grotesquely improbable, no doubt, but still just conceivable? Might the whole story of the cataleptic Russian and his son be a concoction of Dr. Trevelyan's, who has, for his own purposes, been in Blessington's rooms?"

I saw in the gaslight that Holmes wore an amused smile at this brilliant departure of mine.

"My dear fellow," said he, "it was one of the first solutions which occurred to me, but I was soon able to corroborate the doctor's tale. This young man has left prints upon the stair-carpet which made it quite superfluous for me to ask to see those which he had made in the room. When I tell you that his shoes were square-toed instead of being pointed like Blessington's, and were quite an inch and a third longer than the doctor's, you will acknowledge that there can be no doubt as to his individuality. But we may sleep on it now, for I shall be surprised if we do not hear something further from Brook Street in the morning."

Sherlock Holmes's prophecy was soon fulfilled, and in a dramatic fashion. At half-past seven next morning, in the first glimmer of daylight, I found him standing by my bedside in his dressing-gown.

"There's a brougham waiting for us, Watson," said he.

"What's the matter, then?"

"The Brook Street business."

"Any fresh news?"

"Tragic, but ambiguous," said he, pulling up the blind. "Look at this — a sheet from a note-book, with 'For God's sake come at once — P. T.,' scrawled upon it in pencil. Our friend, the doctor, was hard put to it when he wrote this. Come along, my dear fellow, for it's an urgent call."

In a quarter of an hour or so we were back at the physician's house. He came running out to meet us with a face of horror.

"Oh, such a business!" he cried, with his hands to his temples.

"What then?"

"Blessington has committed suicide!"

Holmes whistled.

"Yes, he hanged himself during the night."

We had entered, and the doctor had preceded us into what was evidently his waiting-room.

"I really hardly know what I am doing," he cried. "The police are already upstairs. It has shaken me most dreadfully."

"When did you find it out?"

"He has a cup of tea taken in to him early every morning. When the maid entered, about seven, there the unfortunate fellow was hanging in the middle of the room. He had tied his cord to the hook on which the heavy lamp used to hang, and he had jumped off from the top of the very box that he showed us yesterday."

Holmes stood for a moment in deep thought.

"With your permission," said he at last, "I should like to go upstairs and look into the matter."

We both ascended, followed by the doctor.

It was a dreadful sight which met us as we entered the bedroom door. I have spoken of the impression of flabbiness which this man Blessington conveyed. As he dangled from the hook it was exaggerated and intensified until he was scarce human in his appearance. The neck was drawn out like a plucked chicken's, making the rest of him seem the more obese and unnatural by the contrast. He was clad only in his long night-dress, and his swollen ankles and ungainly feet protruded starkly from beneath it. Beside him stood a smart-looking police-inspector, who was taking notes in a pocket-book.

"Ah, Mr. Holmes," said he, heartily, as my friend entered, "I am delighted to see you."

"Good-morning, Lanner," answered Holmes; "you won't think me an intruder, I am sure. Have you heard of the events which led up to this affair?"

"Yes, I heard something of them."

"Have you formed any opinion?"

"As far as I can see, the man has been driven out of his senses by fright. The bed has been well slept in, you see. There's his impression deep enough. It's about five in the morning, you know, that suicides are most common. That would be about his time for hanging himself. It seems to have been a very deliberate affair."

"I should say that he has been dead about three hours, judging by the rigidity of the muscles," said I.

"Noticed anything peculiar about the room?" asked Holmes.

"Found a screw-driver and some screws on the wash-hand stand. Seems to have smoked heavily during the night, too. Here are four cigar-ends that I picked out of the fireplace."

"Hum!" said Holmes, "have you got his cigar-holder?"

"No, I have seen none."

"His cigar-case, then?"

"Yes, it was in his coat-pocket."

Holmes opened it and smelled the single cigar which it contained.

"Oh, this is an Havana, and these others are cigars of the peculiar sort which are imported by the Dutch from their East Indian colonies. They are usually wrapped in straw, you know, and are thinner for their length than any other brand." He picked up the four ends and examined them with his pocket-lens.

"Two of these have been smoked from a holder and two without," said he. "Two have been cut by a not very sharp knife, and two have had the ends bitten off by a set of excellent teeth. This is no suicide, Mr. Lanner. It is a very deeply planned and cold-blooded murder."

"Impossible!" cried the inspector.

"And why?"

"Why should any one murder a man in so clumsy a fashion as by hanging him?"

"That is what we have to find out."

"How could they get in?"

"Through the front door."

"It was barred in the morning."

"Then it was barred after them."

"How do you know?"

"I saw their traces. Excuse me a moment, and I may be able to give you some further information about it."

He went over to the door, and turning the lock he examined it in his methodical way. Then he took out the key, which was on the inside, and inspected that also. The bed, the carpet, the chairs the mantelpiece, the dead body, and the rope were each in turn examined, until at last he professed himself satisfied, and with my aid and that of the inspector cut down the wretched object and laid it reverently under a sheet.

"How about this rope?" he asked.

"It is cut off this," said Dr. Trevelyan, drawing a large coil from under the bed. "He was morbidly nervous of fire, and always kept this beside him, so that he might escape by the window in case the stairs were burning."

"That must have saved them trouble," said Holmes, thoughtfully. "Yes, the actual facts are very plain, and I shall be surprised if by the afternoon I cannot give you the reasons for them as well. I will take this photograph of Blessington, which I see upon the mantelpiece, as it may help me in my inquiries."

"But you have told us nothing!" cried the doctor.

"Oh, there can be no doubt as to the sequence of events," said Holmes. "There were three of them in it: the young man, the old man, and a third, to whose identity I have no clue. The first two, I need hardly remark, are the same who masqueraded as the Russian count and his son, so we can give a very full description of them. They were admitted by a confederate inside the house. If I might offer you a word of advice, Inspector, it would be to arrest the page, who, as I understand, has only recently come into your service, Doctor."

"The young imp cannot be found," said Dr. Trevelyan; "the maid and the cook have just been searching for him."

Holmes shrugged his shoulders.

"He has played a not unimportant part in this drama," said he. "The three men having ascended the stairs, which they did on tiptoe, the elder man first, the younger man second, and the unknown man in the rear —"

"My dear Holmes!" I ejaculated.

"Oh, there could be no question as to the superimposing of the footmarks. I had the advantage of learning which was which last night. They ascended, then, to Mr. Blessington's room, the door of which they found to be locked. With the help of a wire, however, they forced round the key. Even without the lens you will perceive, by the scratches on this ward, where the pressure was applied.

"On entering the room their first proceeding must have been to gag Mr. Blessington. He may have been asleep, or he may have been so paralysed with terror as to have been unable to cry out. These walls are thick, and it is conceivable that his shriek, if he had time to utter one, was unheard.

"Having secured him, it is evident to me that a consultation of some sort was held. Probably it was something in the nature of a judicial proceeding. It must have lasted for some time, for it was then that these cigars were smoked. The older man sat in that wicker chair; it was he who used the cigar-holder. The younger man sat over yonder; he knocked his ash off against the chest of drawers. The third fellow paced up and down. Blessington, I think, sat upright in the bed, but of that I cannot be absolutely certain.

"Well, it ended by their taking Blessington and hanging him. The matter was so prearranged that it is my belief that they brought with them some sort of block or pulley which might serve as a gallows. That screw-driver and those screws were, as I conceive, for fixing it up. Seeing the hook, however they naturally saved themselves the trouble. Having finished their work they made off, and the door was barred behind them by their confederate."

We had all listened with the deepest interest to this sketch of the night's doings, which Holmes had deduced from signs so subtle and minute that, even when he had pointed them out to us, we could scarcely follow him in his reasoning. The inspector hurried away on the instant to make inquiries about the page, while Holmes and I returned to Baker Street for breakfast.

"I'll be back by three," said he, when we had finished our meal. "Both the inspector and the doctor will meet me here at that hour, and I hope by that time to have cleared up any little obscurity which the case may still present."

Our visitors arrived at the appointed time, but it was a quarter to four before my friend put in an appearance. From his expression as he entered, however, I could see that all had gone well with him.

"Any news, Inspector?"

"We have got the boy, sir."

"Excellent, and I have got the men."

"You have got them!" we cried, all three.

"Well, at least I have got their identity. This so-called Blessington is, as I expected, well known at headquarters, and so are his assailants. Their names are Biddle, Hayward, and Moffat."

"The Worthingdon bank gang," cried the inspector.

"Precisely," said Holmes.

"Then Blessington must have been Sutton."

"Exactly," said Holmes.

"Why, that makes it as clear as crystal," said the inspector.

But Trevelyan and I looked at each other in bewilderment.

"You must surely remember the great Worthingdon bank business," said Holmes. "Five men were in it — these four and a fifth called Cartwright. Tobin, the care-taker, was murdered, and the thieves got away with seven thousand pounds. This was in 1875. They were all five arrested, but the evidence against them was by no means conclusive. This Blessington or Sutton, who was the worst of the gang, turned informer. On his evidence Cartwright was hanged and the other three got fifteen years apiece. When they got out the other day, which was some years before their full term, they set themselves, as you perceive, to hunt down the traitor and to avenge the death of their comrade upon him. Twice they tried to get at him and failed; a third time, you see, it came off. Is there anything further which I can explain, Dr. Trevelyan?"

"I think you have made it all remarkable clear," said the doctor. "No doubt the day on which he was perturbed was the day when he had seen of their release in the newspapers."

"Quite so. His talk about a burglary was the merest blind."

"But why could he not tell you this?"

"Well, my dear sir, knowing the vindictive character of his old associates, he was trying to hide his own identity from everybody as long as he could. His secret was a shameful one, and he could not bring himself to divulge it. However, wretch as he was, he was still living under the shield of British law, and I have no doubt, Inspector, that you will see that, though that shield may fail to guard, the sword of justice is still there to avenge."

Such were the singular circumstances in connection with the Resident Patient and the Brook Street Doctor. From that night nothing has been seen of the three murderers by the police, and it is surmised at Scotland Yard that they were among the passengers of the ill-fated steamer Norah Creina, which was lost some years ago with all hands upon the Portuguese coast, some leagues to the north of Oporto. The proceedings against the page broke down for want of evidence, and the Brook Street Mystery, as it was called, has never until now been fully dealt with in any public print.

✗

YOU ARE MY SHERLOCK

(OR DOCTOR WATSON'S LAMENT)

by Len Moffatt

The other night, Holmes,
While you were sleuthing
I dreamed of all our calls to arms.
When I awoke, Holmes,
I had misgivings
And I hung my head and sighed.

You are my Sherlock,
My only Sherlock.
Your cases earn me
An author's pay.
You'll never know, Holmes,
How much I need you—
Please don't take my Sherlock away

You called me once, Holmes,
Your "Good Old Watson!"
Oh, how we shared mutual esteem!
But now you tell me
You are retiring—
You have shattered all my dreams!

You are my Sherlock,
My only Sherlock.
I can't believe
You will not stay!
You're leaving me, Holmes—
For bees in Sussex?
Please don't take my Sherlock away!

Made in the USA
Lexington, KY
31 May 2012